MIRACLE ON LADIES' MILE

A GILDED AGE HOLIDAY NOVELLA

JOANNA SHUPE

Copyright © 2017 by Joanna Shupe

Originally published in the 2016 *Christmas in America* anthology.

All rights reserved.

No part of this book may be reproduced in any form or by any electronic or mechanical means, including information storage and retrieval systems, without written permission from the author, except for the use of brief quotations in a book review.

*To anyone who has ever struggled
to make ends meet...*

"To the everlasting credit of New York's working-girl let it be said that, rough though her road may be, all but hopeless her battle with life, only in the rarest instances does she go astray. As a class she is brave, virtuous, and true."
—Jacob Riis, *How the Other Half Lives*, 1890.

CHAPTER 1

NEW YORK CITY, 1895

A man was watching her from the other side of the glass.

Grace did her best to ignore the tall, well-dressed stranger and focus on her task. She'd been hired four weeks ago at McCall & Armstrong's—or Mac & Arm's as it was often called—to assist with designing Christmas window displays. Mac & Arm's was *the* finest department store in New York City, catering to the very best clientele. Her boss, Mr. Bernard, would not be pleased if Grace failed to complete this window tonight.

"Finish this all before you leave, Miss Shipley," Mr. Bernard had said in a French accent, though she knew he hailed from Poughkeepsie. "Remember, exactly as I have sketched it out for you. *Exactement.*" As if she didn't already know the plans intimately. She had drawn the rough draft of each window design, after all.

Christmas was less than a month away. Eight displays needed to be installed in the next few days. This would be the first year for holiday windows at Mac & Arm's, and Mr. McCall had overseen many of the details himself. He seemed like a nice man, and it was easy to see why he'd been successful in business. Rumor held Mr. Armstrong was pricklier, which must explain why he kept to the top floor. Grace hadn't ever met the man. Instead, Mr. McCall routinely dealt with the store's staff.

The job had been interesting thus far, putting her love of color and fabric to good use. The designs were based on Hans Christian Andersen's fairy tales, with each window representing a different story. The pieces were being finished downstairs in the basement and, as the only staff member without a family to go home to, Grace had been asked to assemble those pieces in the windows themselves.

She wiped the beads of sweat from her brow. Small and cramped, the window boxes had poor ventilation. Brown paper covered the glass, which made it a bit like standing in a burlap sack. However, it was late, after the store had closed, so she hadn't seen the harm in peeling back a section of said brown paper to see the vibrant city surrounding the Twenty-Third Street store.

New York City never stopped moving, its pace endlessly fascinating, and Grace hated to miss a minute of the excitement. Someday, after she'd saved enough, she would be part of that chaos, going to dinner here and shows there. Dancing at the Haymarket. Shopping Ladies' Mile. But for now, her view of the city at night was through one small missing section in the brown paper.

Unfortunately, thanks to this small opening, a man was now observing her from the sidewalk.

He'd been looming there for at least two minutes. Dressed in a well-fitted black coat, he held a brown leather satchel in one hand, the other wrapped around the silver handle of an ebony cane. A derby sat perched on a head full of brown hair. He didn't smile, wink, or even nod at her. He just observed her with an intensity that would've made her nervous under other circumstances...such as, if she weren't encased in a safe—albeit hot—glass tomb.

Why was he there? Perhaps he worked for Macy's or Lord & Taylor's and had decided to size up the competition. Well, she couldn't help that now. He'd already seen the contents of the window, so it hardly made sense to cover the glass back up. The best thing to do would be to finish quickly and leave for the night. If she were taken to task in the morning for revealing the windows to a competitor, then she'd own up to it.

A lie weights down your soul, her mother used to say.

She decided to ignore him and concentrate on the next item on her to-do list: assemble the lily pads. She collected the pieces and approached the small pond she'd created on the right side of the display. They had used a shallow round tub to hold the water, with metal poles coming up from the bottom to lift the lily pads.

Bending, she began to fit the poles together. When the last two lily pads remained, she sighed. Her arms weren't long enough to reach the empty poles. "Rats," she muttered. Really, why on earth hadn't she waited to fill the tub until *after* the lily pads were installed? This was why she much preferred drawing and planning than executing the designs.

Grace carefully climbed onto the edge of the pond, raising her skirts to keep them out of the water. She put a hand to the wall to steady herself as she shuffled her feet, but she misjudged the lip of the tub on her next step. Off-balance, she wobbled for a few seconds before her right foot dropped into the water. The leather of her shoe instantly soaked through, all the way down to her woolen stockings, chilling her skin.

"Double rats." *Nothing to be done for it now.* Grace shivered and then remembered her audience. Had he...?

Her head snapped up. The man was still there, his dark eyes round and lips parted in surprise. She shifted and water squelched out of her boot. No wonder he was staring at her like that. She must look an absolute fool.

She laughed. Unsurprising that she'd fallen into the water; her clumsiness was legendary in the Shipley family. And of course, a handsome stranger had witnessed this debacle. Didn't that perfectly sum up Grace's romantic life?

You can't always be perfect, so be genuine instead.

Grace had taken her grandmother's advice to heart, both in relationships and her art. So instead of cowering in embarrassment, she locked eyes with the man on the other side of the glass and gave a proper curtsy.

No laugh. No smile. Instead, he blinked a few times, spun on his heel, and strode out of her line of sight.

Disappointed, but not surprised, she climbed out of the pond and tried to wring out her skirts. Removing her boot was impossible while fully dressed, so she stomped the wet foot to remove some of the moisture. *Every path has a few puddles.* Goodness, Grace never thought she'd experience that bit of family wisdom literally.

Water had dripped onto the floor, but thankfully none of the display pieces were ruined. Yet. She needed to find a way to quickly clean up the mess. This window display had to be completed tonight. She couldn't risk losing her position.

This job was the first step in her life plan. One day, she'd be the most popular dressmaker in all of New York. She'd been crafting her own clothes for years, and a career in clothing design was her dream. Getting fired meant never working her way up higher in the Mac & Arm's dress design department.

The door in the rear of the display suddenly opened, startling her. The man from the sidewalk appeared. How on earth had he gotten inside the store? Had the guards let him in?

He held out a new cloth. "Here." His voice was deep, the one word said with authority. Grace's stomach flipped.

"Did you take that off the store's shelf?" was all she could think to say.

He tilted his head, and the lines on his brow deepened. "Yes."

"Then I cannot use it. That's stealing." Never mind that she desperately needed a towel. However, she couldn't use anything belonging to the store. She hadn't a way to pay for it.

He opened his mouth, and then closed it. His expression grew even more perplexed. "Do not worry. I'll cover the cost. Please, take it."

"You'll cover it, how? The store is closed."

"I'll pay for it tomorrow."

Ah, so he did work here. That explained why the night guard had allowed him inside. "That is not necessary. I'll pay for the towel." Somehow. She'd figure it out. Perhaps Mr. Bernard would agree to an advance on her wages.

He stepped farther into the box. In the electric light, she could see that his brown eyes were actually hazel with a hint of green. He was striking this close up. So striking that she felt flustered. His handsomeness was not the romantic, classical kind, soft and gentle, the type reserved for actors and poets. Instead, it was like a punch to the solar plexus. As if you were standing in the presence of a fine marble statue, art so beautiful and raw it stole your breath.

And he saw you fall into the pool. He feels sorry for you.

"Miss...?"

"Shipley."

"Miss Shipley, I promise to compensate the store for the cloth."

"Cross your heart?"

The harsh lines of his face eased, as if she amused him. "Yes, cross my heart. I'll pay for the cloth first thing in the morning."

Normally she didn't accept gifts from strangers, especially men, but it seemed like an exception could be made in this case. "Fine." She closed the distance between them and accepted the soft cotton. "If you forget, send a note to the design department. I'll work something out with Mr. Bernard as far as payment."

He gave a brisk nod. "I'll leave you to it. Good night."

Dawn hadn't yet broken when Alexander Armstrong entered his office at the usual time the following morning. He'd carefully avoided passing the holiday windows. She wouldn't still be there, of course, but he didn't need another reminder of her.

She'd fallen into a pond...and laughed.

He could have watched her all night.

She had one of those expressive faces where every thought and feeling was written clear across it. And freckles, for God's sake. When was the last time he'd seen a woman with freckles on her nose? The women he knew hated the sun and took every precaution against the outside elements.

The surprises hadn't stopped there. Miss Shipley possessed lush curves instead of a willowy figure. Clear, guileless blue eyes, and a smile that transformed her from passably pretty into breathtaking.

She was an adorable guppy in a sea of bloodthirsty sharks. A bolt of pure sunshine in a city that thrived in the dark.

Alex also thrived in the dark. His soul had rotted years ago . . . seven to be precise. Grown over with weeds and brush, untended and deserted. Such was what happened when joy abruptly departed. Shaking off the bad memories, he clicked the chain to turn on the lights, removed his frock coat, and rolled up his sleeves. *Time to work.*

Hours later, a knock sounded on his door. "Yes?"

Gerald McCall, Alex's business partner, stepped inside the room. "Good morning. Do you have a moment?"

Alex placed his pen in the holder. "Of course. Would you care to sit?"

Gerald lowered himself into the chair opposite Alex's desk and crossed his legs. "What happened to Miss Neely?"

"Who?"

"Your secretary."

"Oh. She quit yesterday."

Silence stretched. He could feel the weight of Gerald's disapproval. Alex didn't try to run his secretaries off, but the longest he'd managed to keep one had been six weeks. True, he liked things a certain way. Organized. Efficient. In the five years since they started Mac & Arm's, not one secretary had done the job according to his precise instructions. They called him "gruff" and "demanding"—right before they quit.

"I'll have Pauline call the service again," Gerald said, referring to his own long-time secretary. "Now, have you given any more thought to Philadelphia?"

"I'm not certain Philadelphia is the right location for expansion. Wanamaker's and Gimbel's already have the city sewn up."

"Not in the luxury market. There's nothing quite like Mac & Arm's there. And the property at Eleventh and Market won't be available much longer."

Alex tapped his fingers on the desk. Gerald liked to take risks, while he managed things more conservatively. It was one reason their partnership worked. But lately, Alex felt as if he was doing most of the bending. "How much are you spending on these holiday windows again?"

"We're back to arguing about the windows? I told you, they will bring people into the store."

"Wrong. They'll bring people to the *outside* of the store. It remains to be seen whether those people will come inside to purchase anything."

Gerald held up his hands. "True, but we can't let Macy's outdo us. Soon, everyone in New York will follow suit with holiday window displays. Mark my words."

"We'll see, I suppose. Remember what happens if we don't see at least a twenty percent sales bump."

"How could I forget when you remind me at every turn? And, I agreed. No more money toward the window displays if the revenue doesn't increase."

"At least twenty percent," Alex repeated. "Colossal waste of resources, in my opinion. Incidentally, who is the woman Bernard hired to assist with the windows?"

The change in topic appeared to confuse Gerald. He frowned. "The woman? Oh, the young girl. A Miss Shiplow, I think."

"Shipley," Alex corrected. "I meant, what do you know about her? And why is she assembling the windows by herself in the wee hours of the night? Shouldn't Bernard be there as well?"

"Yes, I had thought he would stay. I know he's busy with Christmas orders but that's no excuse to shirk the duties of the windows. I'll visit today and see how they are faring."

"Please do. It's unsafe for her to be there alone at such an hour." He could still see her, struggling and sweating, one woman doing the job of five strong men.

Cross your heart? The words, as well as the earnest delivery, had stayed with him. No one had ever asked him to do such a silly thing, not even his daughter, Sarah, and Miss Shipley hadn't been kidding.

One thing he knew, he would die before not making good on that promise.

"I see." Gerald's lips curled into an annoying smile.

"No, there is nothing to see," Alex snapped. Reaching into his vest pocket, he withdrew a few coins. "Please have these delivered to the furnishing department. I took a bath towel off the shelf last night."

Gerald pocketed the coins. "A bath towel? What on earth did you require one for?"

"To soak up water."

When Alex didn't elaborate, Gerald pushed out of the chair. "So... Philadelphia? May I tell the lawyers to purchase the land and have the architects draw up the plans? Or, should we continue to discuss bath towels and your need for them in the middle of the—?"

"Fine, I'll look into the Philadelphia proposal further today." Anything so Gerald would leave him alone and cease with his probing questions.

Gerald smiled and started to leave, then turned around abruptly. "You know, Alex, it wouldn't be the worst thing in the world if a young woman caught your eye. Mary has been gone for seven years. You're only thirty. Isn't it about time—"

"No."

Just *no*. There was no replacing Mary. She was not a pocket watch or an umbrella stand. She had been the light, the sun. The beacon of happiness that had lit him up from within. His *everything*.

They had met as kids—practically babies, really. But he hadn't noticed her until the summer he turned seventeen. Mary had been sixteen, draped in a long white dress. A beautiful blond angel who'd stood up to sing in the church choir. He'd never heard a voice as lovely as Mary's, strong and pure. It had carried over the rows of people and prayer books to punch him square in the gut. He'd fallen in love with her right there, knew in his bones she was the girl with whom he'd spend the rest of his life.

He'd been wrong, tragically so. By the time he finished school and proposed, he'd been twenty and foolish enough to think they had all the time in the world. Fifty-two short months they'd been married. Not even five years before cancer had stolen her from him.

He hadn't yet recovered from Mary's death. Hell, he didn't *want* to recover. He had Mac & Arm's and Sarah, his daughter. *Mary's* daughter. That was more than enough.

"Merely think on it. Life is for the living, Alex. It's not meant to be a memorial to the dead."

Alex ignored him and returned to the financial reports on his desk.

CHAPTER 2

He'd returned.

Grace noticed the man right away. Once again, she'd peeled back a small section of the paper covering, enough to see the nighttime sky and deserted streets while she worked. Tonight's window was *The Little Mermaid*, complete with sand and seashells brought in from Long Island.

Sweat had just started to roll down her temples when her Knight of the Dry Bath Towels had arrived to stand on the walk and scowl at her.

Just as the night before, a strange fluttering sensation blossomed in her chest. His derby was pulled low, framing greenish-brown eyes that glowed fierce in the lamplight. Actually, *fierce* pretty much described every part of him. Hollowed-out cheekbones and an unforgiving, clean-shaven jaw. A strong nose. Wide shoulders and long limbs. Neither graceful nor soft, he reminded her of a fascinating storm, one that dared you to jump off the front porch and dance in the rain, no matter how dangerous.

They often had storms like that at home in Pennsylvania, and Grace loved being outside when they came—much to her mother's dismay. She had insisted Grace would be carried away by the winds

Miracle On Ladies' Mile

one day. *Better to die living than die watching,* Grace had countered, to which Mama only shook her head.

But men were not storms. This was not Pennsylvania. Strange men on the street were not always friendly, and she had no idea why he'd returned to the window. So she ignored him and continued to work. There were hundreds of seashells that needed to be positioned *"just so,"* according to Mr. Bernard.

A minute later, a tap on the glass caught her attention. Heart pounding like the rattle of the elevated train, she met his hazel gaze. "Yes?"

"Why are you here alone?" he asked, his voice muffled through the thick pane separating them. "Who is supposed to be helping you?"

Helping her? Mr. Bernard had left well over two hours ago. "No one is supposed to be here except me."

That answer displeased him for some reason. The lines bracketing his mouth deepened. Transferring his satchel to his other hand, he spun on his heel and disappeared. Both disappointment and relief rolled through her, which made absolutely no sense whatsoever.

She returned to her task, her mind still on the man. He clearly worked in the store but she hadn't seen him today. Not that she'd searched...much. Merely every second she hadn't been entombed in the basement with Mr. Bernard. The store clerks always departed en masse at closing time, so her visitor must hold a position in the stock room or the shipping department. *Little well dressed for that, wasn't he?*

Grace knew fabrics and stitching, and his suit had been expensively crafted. Even still, this could mean any number of things. She'd learned not to judge others by what they wore. One of the heiresses who routinely shopped at Mac & Arm's wore an oversized sackcloth dress as if Charles Frederick Worth himself had designed it.

The door at the rear of the display flew open. A long leg clad in striped navy wool stepped in, quickly followed by the rest of his frame. It was the man from the street. He'd removed his derby and overcoat.

Grace gaped at him. "What do you think you're doing?"

"Helping you."

He started unbuttoning his frock coat. Her mouth went as dry as dust. He was too big, the space too small, her mind too frazzled. "Helping me with what?"

"The display." He shrugged out of the coat and tossed it into the store. Then he removed his cuff links and slipped them in his pocket. "You'll be finished sooner this way."

True, but that didn't explain why he felt compelled to intercede. And why was he removing his clothing? She watched as he rolled up his sleeves, revealing sinewy forearms lightly covered with dark hair. Muscles shifted as he worked, tendons rippling with movement, and heat unfurled in her lower body. Her pulse shot higher than one of the city's new skyscrapers.

Had she ever noticed a man's forearms before? These seemed exemplary specimens. Just outstanding. Strong and seductive, with veins clearly visible under the golden skin. If there were a museum for forearms he could donate his for posterity. *But then he would be dead, Grace.*

Confused and disturbed by her thoughts, she turned away. There was not enough air in this box. She fanned herself with her hand. "That's unnecessary. I am able to manage."

"Why is it so damn hot in here?"

Because you are removing your clothing.

She should tell him to leave. Call the night guard. Cover her eyes. Do something. Yet she somehow knew he wouldn't hurt her. He'd brought her a towel last night, after all, and promised to pay for it. This was just one Mac & Arm's employee helping another. Besides, a man this handsome wouldn't be interested in *her*. No doubt he had a beautiful wife and a few kids at home. Probably a dog, too.

Grace had a single room in a boarding house, the only company being a few spiders that lived in the cabinet above her sink.

She picked up another handful of seashells. "There's no air flow, unfortunately. If you fear small spaces, I won't judge you for leaving."

"I'm not leaving, and I don't fear small places. I do, however, fear dying of asphyxiation. Why do you keep the door shut?"

"Mr. Bernard doesn't want the crowds peeking into the windows. I guess I forgot to open it after the store closed. Not that it much helps. The air doesn't move in here."

"Tell me what to do."

"Well, Mr.... That's funny. I don't know your name."

"Alex. Just Alex."

Oh. They were to be on a first-name basis? That seemed rather forward, but she supposed the polite thing to do would be to follow suit. Most of the employees in the store were on a first-name basis anyway. "Nice to meet you. I'm Grace."

He studied her, his head tilted slightly. "Grace. The name fits you."

The husky, low tone scraped over her skin like a fine-toothed comb, producing gooseflesh everywhere. Inhaling deeply, she steeled herself. He hadn't been flirting with her, merely commenting. The reaction had all been in her head.

She forced a snort to keep the mood light. "Hardly. I'm the clumsiest person I know."

"Doubtful, but let's not argue before we start. What can I do to help?"

Yes, the work. They needed to focus on the work. "Well, I need to spread these shells. Then I'll hang the fabric from the ceiling."

"Why don't I hang while you spread?" He glanced about. "Where is your stepladder?"

"By the door? Mr. Bernard promised he would bring it up from the basement for me."

A muscle worked in Alex's jaw. "There's no stepladder there."

"Oh. I suppose I'll need to go down—"

"I'll get it."

Alex was out the door before she could stop him. Did he know the way to the basement? She thought about going after him, offering to help, but he seemed confident, a man used to doing things for himself. And why did she find that so appealing?

Married, kids, dog, she reminded herself. Surely some other woman had the right to admire those forearms. Exhaling, Grace returned to her task and tried to gather her wits before he returned.

The basement smelled of paint and drudgery.

Alex took in the haphazardly organized space—cloth strewn about, jars of paints on their side, ribbons and canvases tossed any which way—and cursed. How could a person get any work done down here? The place was a mess. He made a mental note to instruct Gerald to deal with this first thing in the morning. An office should be always arranged neatly, even a basement.

And why was it so blasted hot down here? There were windows—not many, but a few, high up enough as to be impervious to thieves. So why weren't they open?

What really irritated Alex was the absence of another employee in those display windows tonight. Grace was all alone—again—designing and sweating, while the other workers—specifically Mr. Bernard—relaxed at home. How was that fair?

He located the stepladder behind a stack of dirty cloths. A few minutes and one flight of stairs later, he brought the ladder into the display window. Grace turned at his entrance and gave him a wide, bright smile, one that transformed her entire face. Alex felt his chest flutter like some dime novel heroine. *Christ.*

However embarrassing, the visceral response could not be helped. When was the last time a woman had looked at him as if he had crossed mountains and slain dragons for her? *Not since Mary.*

He turned away. He did not want that reminder, not now. He remembered Mary often enough each time he saw his daughter's face. The governess couldn't understand why Alex didn't spend more time with Sarah, why he worked constantly, even on Sunday. But to see Sarah was like seeing Mary, and Alex couldn't quite manage it. Perhaps in a few years, after the pain had lessened a bit.

You're a coward.

He opened the stepladder, securing it. "There you are."

Miracle On Ladies' Mile

"Thank you. I didn't ask if you knew your way to the basement, but clearly you do." She held out the fabric that would drape the ceiling.

He took the cloth and climbed up the ladder. She presented him with a ceramic jar filled with pins. "Here, you'll need these as well."

"Just pin it up here? How?"

"Drape it like waves."

Waves? Alex stared at the ceiling, trying to imagine how to accomplish this impossible design feat.

His confusion must have shown because she said, "I have an idea. Why don't you spread shells while I pin the fabric? I've draped fabric before. It'll be easier for me."

He didn't argue. Obviously, the fabric was the more physically demanding task, but it would be slower and more difficult for her to hover by his side telling him how to do it.

Coming down from the ladder, he secured the wood with his hands and held it steady. Grace climbed up, her brown skirts in one fist to keep from tripping, and Alex caught a flash of shapely calf covered by cream-colored stockings as she ascended. He swallowed hard, knowing he should look away and not wanting to, and a hot prickling sensation washed over his skin.

What was wrong with him? There had been women since Mary's death. The first time had been difficult, like ripping a scab from not-quite-healed skin, but it had grown easier over the years. Sexual release was a necessary function of being an adult man, along the lines of shaving or keeping his shoes shined, and there reached a point where his hand hadn't been enough. So he'd sought out willing partners. He took them to a hotel for a few hours with the promise of mutual pleasure and nothing permanent. He'd had permanent once, the very best kind, and he had no intention of ever repeating it.

So there was no reason for this one woman to burrow into his brain like quarterly earnings reports. To be *memorable* in any way. Yet his eyes remained glued to her legs, his mind praying for a rogue wind to infiltrate this blasted death chamber and reward him.

Now on the top step, she settled her skirts and covered herself.

Pathetically disappointed, Alex cleared his throat and shifted his gaze to her face. She stared at the ceiling the way a general examined a field before battle.

"There is no need to hold the stepladder," she informed him. "I won't fall."

"Which is precisely what one says...right before he or she falls."

Her head tilted as her brows lowered. "Are you, by chance, an expert at designing holiday windows?"

"No, absolutely not."

"Well, you might dictate things in whichever of the store's departments you work, but here, in this window, I dictate what happens. Let go of the stepladder and finish up the shells, please."

Alex felt his lips twitch, a smile eager to break free. He couldn't remember the last time he'd been so thoroughly put in his place. From anyone else, he'd have balked at that treatment, but Grace...

He stepped back, hands in the air. "As you wish."

Twenty minutes later, he had to concede to her brilliance. The way she twisted and gathered the fabric truly caused the ceiling to appear like waves. Of course, he'd kept close in case she toppled— not that he'd ever admit it to her.

As she moved the ladder to complete her last section of ceiling, he heard himself ask, "Have you always wanted to design holiday windows?" He nearly winced. Was he actually making polite small talk? God, Gerald would piss himself laughing if he'd heard.

"Goodness, no. I didn't even know there was such a thing. I do enjoy it, though. Mr. Bernard has been very kind to listen to my ideas."

That news might have just saved Bernard's job. "Is that so?"

She nodded. "Yes, he agreed the fairy tales were a good way to appeal to both children and parents."

Alex straightened, shells in his hand forgotten. *Agreed?* "Wait, are you saying the idea to use the Hans Christian Andersen fairy tales was yours?"

"I might've mentioned it first but we discussed the ideas as a group."

Miracle On Ladies' Mile 17

She was being gracious. Women were bred that way, but Alex would bet his last dollar Bernard had taken Grace's vision and claimed it as his own. Had probably forced Grace to do most of the work on building the display pieces as well.

He would speak to Gerald about this and have his partner get to the bottom of what had happened. Alex believed in giving credit to those who deserved it, not stealing from someone else and using the idea as your own.

"In which part of the store do you work?"

He realized he'd been silent awhile, thinking, as he continued with the shells. Grace was merely making a polite inquiry to pass the time, but he liked that she didn't know his real identity. He hadn't been plain Alex in a long while. With Grace, he wasn't part owner in one of the biggest retail companies in the eastern United States. Or even the wealthy widower Alexander Armstrong, for whom match-making mamas laid in wait at every event. The anonymity was freeing.

So he lied.

"I work in a variety of places. It differs by day."

Exhaling, she pushed another pin into the fabric. "That must be nice. Which department is your favorite?"

He didn't even need to think on an answer. "Furs."

At twenty years of age, Alex had been hired as an accountant in Gerald's fur store on Canal Street. He'd shown an aptitude for the fur business and worked his way up to vice-president. When Gerald had come to him with the idea to start Mac & Arm's five years ago, Alex had jumped at the chance.

"Truly? You don't strike me as a man who would enjoy soft, luxurious things."

Instead of sable and mink, her words conjured images of supple, creamy skin. Plush thighs and curves that cushioned a man's hips. Legs that wound around his back, holding him tight while he pleasured them both. Yes, he very much enjoyed soft, luxurious things.

Grace's skin would undoubtedly feel as silky as it looked. He would love to trace it with his tongue...

Dear God. He was hardening inside his clothing, his shaft increasing at the idea of taking this young, fresh-faced woman to bed. What was she doing to him?

Movement dragged his attention back to the window display. Grace had begun descending the ladder, so he stepped closer in case she required assistance. Before he could get there, however, her boot slipped off a rung and she started to fall.

CHAPTER 3

Grace's teeth clacked when her foot slipped off the rung. Her body was thrown off balance as she tilted backward. *Oh, no,* she thought. Her hands searched for purchase to stop the inevitable.

Before she toppled to the ground, strong arms caught her around the waist. "I've got you," a deep, soothing voice rumbled behind her. "Take a deep breath. You're fine."

Startled, all she could do was stay there. Her heart raced while she recovered. After several long seconds, she noticed other things, like how his torso pressed tightly to her back. How powerful his arms felt wrapped around her middle. His warm hands stroking idly over her corseted ribs. The rapid rise and fall of his chest, the breath caressing the nape of her neck. He didn't let her go and she didn't try to move.

She relaxed, allowed her lids to close, and melted into his larger frame. *If heaven could be bottled in a feeling, this was it right here.* Capable and solid, he surrounded her, and the scent of soap and musk filled her nose. When was the last time she'd felt this safe, this protected? Not since moving to New York City, that was for certain.

He dragged in a deep lungful of air near her ear. Was he smelling her, too? Tingles broke out over her skin, excitement shooting along her spine. Suddenly, Grace realized how unappealing she must appear at the moment. Sweaty and dirty, reeking of turpentine. Not to mention her perpetual clumsiness around this man.

Horror overtook everything else rattling around in her brain. She stiffened. "Thank you for catching me."

Taking the hint, he disengaged his arms and stepped away. "Of course." Had his voice been quite that husky earlier?

An awkward silence descended. Her hand trembled as she smoothed her hair in place.

"Now what?" His hands pushed into his trouser pockets.

"The only two remaining tasks are to hang seaweed from the ceiling and assemble our mermaid."

"How about I take the seaweed?"

The unspoken *"since you almost fell off the ladder before"* hung between them. Considering how jittery she still felt from his embrace, the decision didn't bother her. "That's probably for the best." She set him up with the seaweed pieces and the pins, directed him on what she wanted, then went to work on positioning the mermaid.

While her hands remained busy, her eyes wandered to where he leaned on the stepladder. Alex worked carefully, methodically. No wasted effort as he crisscrossed the ceiling in an orderly fashion. The fine fabric of his starched shirt pulled taut as he reached above him, showing off well-developed bicep and shoulder muscles. His vest hugged a trim waist, with trousers draping sturdy legs. Just watching him heated her blood, while the memory of his frame flush with hers caused butterflies in her stomach.

She tried not to stare at other parts of his body, but the window box was tiny and his backside repeatedly drew her attention. If his forearms could be featured in a museum, his backside had her longing for paint and canvas because that particular masculine detail should be immortalized for all eternity. It would be a charitable endeavor, really. Women everywhere would thank her.

"Are you married?" She winced, unsure why she'd asked such a personal thing. "I apologize. I have no right to ask you—"

"No, I'm not married."

His terse answer, laced with emotion, told her this was an uncomfortable question. She opened her mouth to apologize again for bringing it up when he said, "I am a widower."

Sympathy welled in her chest. She knew the pain of losing a loved one, though hers had been a parent. "I am very sorry."

"Thank you." He stepped to the floor and moved the ladder forward. "She died seven years ago."

"That must have been hard."

He made a noise as if to say, *yes, it had been very hard*, and she nearly winced for bringing up such a sensitive topic. "She was young," he said. "We both were. I never expected... Well, I never expected to lose her so soon." He was on the ladder again, hanging seaweed.

Questions burned her tongue and she couldn't seem to prevent herself from asking one. "Had you known her a long time?"

"We grew up together in a small town upstate. We always knew each other, then started getting serious when I turned seventeen."

Goodness, seventeen. "You must have loved her very much." Why did that thought depress her? Just because she was nineteen and hadn't yet fallen in love didn't mean she never would. Her mother always maintained Grace was a late bloomer, like her favorite flower, the sunflower.

Besides, Grace was a city girl now. She had a career and independence. Why would she want to ruin that with a marriage and babies? No, she needed to focus on herself and her goal of becoming a successful clothing designer. Grace would create fancy dresses for the ladies of New York. Her pieces would be coveted everywhere from San Francisco to Bar Harbor. The basement of Mac & Arm's was merely the first stop on her journey upward.

"I did," he said quietly. Grace had to recall what she'd said. Oh, yes. That he'd loved his wife. She concentrated on fitting the pieces of the mermaid together and posing her on the rocks, unsure what to say. Sometimes silence was the best response.

His deep voice continued. "I haven't talked about her for years. Feels strange."

"Why not? I would think talking about her would help you remember."

"Remembering isn't the problem. Also, there comes a point where everyone else moves on with their grief. They expect you to move on as well."

And he hadn't moved past the grief. The poor man. Was that why he looked so grim, so intense? He'd been keeping all his misery bottled up, left to fester inside. "My father always said grief is the price we pay for love."

"Sounds like a wise man, your father."

"He was." Grace's lips curved into a bittersweet smile as she fought the lump in her throat. "He died four months ago."

"My condolences."

"Thank you." Mermaid completed, she straightened, ready to put these morose topics behind them. "There, she's finished. How are you coming with the seaweed?"

He climbed down from the ladder. "Finished as well." His gaze swept the interior. "Well done, Miss Shipley. This window is remarkable."

"You deserve half the credit, but thank you. I would still have a few hours' work ahead of me if it wasn't for your help."

"It was my pleasure." He closed the ladder and carried it to the door in the rear of the display. "Would you care for a ride? I'll hail us a hack. My treat."

A ride? In a tiny carriage? *Alone*? Grace wasn't certain of the propriety or the safety of such an idea. Of course, if this man intended to hurt her there'd been ample opportunity to do so over the last hour. She'd fallen into his arms, for heaven's sake, and nothing had happened.

Besides, a warm carriage sounded like a far better idea than waiting in the cold for a late streetcar, not to mention cheaper.

"Thank you. I'd be grateful for a ride if it's not out of your way."

❄

Miracle On Ladies' Mile 23

The hired carriage rumbled over deserted cobblestone streets in the direction of Grace's boarding house. Conversation had been polite, if not exactly revelatory. Alex wasn't sure what to say to her. She was so young and cheerful, content to watch out the window as if she found every building and storefront fascinating.

Anything he wanted to ask—her age, her favorite hobby, her romantic status—felt wildly inappropriate. Woefully inept at casual conversation with the fairer sex, his experience with women since Mary's death had been limited to questions such as, "Hard and fast, or slow and gentle?"

He brushed the cloth of his trouser leg, smoothing it. Better to remain silent. He had no interest in anything other than a quick fuck, and Grace Shipley, with her freckles and good-natured outlook on life, was not a woman of experience seeking sexual relief. She would undoubtedly expect a wedding ring before engaging in anything physical, and Alex had no intention of marrying again. Ever.

However, he could still help her, at least while she worked at Mac & Arm's. Weren't all the employees his responsibility in some small way? God knew Gerald was always telling him as much. He just hadn't ever acted on it until now, until Grace brought out this strange desire in him to protect her.

He cleared his throat. "Why is your supervisor not assisting you with the windows?"

She turned toward him. Her thigh brushed his, and a streak of heat raced down to his toes. "Mr. Bernard has entrusted the completion of the windows to me."

He scoffed. More like Bernard didn't care to overexert himself by sweating in those tiny glass windows. So Grace had originated the fairy tale concept and assembled the windows. Alex could see what was happening. "What has been Mr. Bernard's role in all this, exactly?"

"Well, he completed the sketches of the windows."

"Completed, meaning he took your drawings and tweaked them?"

"I did some very rough drawings. They needed refinement."

Likely Bernard's word, *refinement*. Alex's opinion of the store's head designer plummeted even further. "From what I can tell, you're very talented—and I don't give praise often." As in ever.

"Thank you. I am learning so much from Mr. Bernard." Alex stifled a snort as she continued. "One day, I hope to design my own dresses for sale at a store like Mac & Arm's."

"Why not open your own shop? House of Shipley."

She laughed, a sound that unwound something inside him. He liked to hear her laugh, the sound genuine and easy, like she did it a lot. "That would be a dream come true. I would be thrilled if women all over the country wore my creations. I must start somewhere, however, and one cannot do better than Mac & Arm's."

An absurd burst of pride went through him at her regard for his store. "Have you designed clothing before?"

She swept a hand over her brown skirt. "Yes, this. I sew all my own clothing."

Visions of undergarments, like lacy satin drawers and silk chemises, floated through his mind. Did she sew those as well? The mere idea caused lust to flare in his gut. He shifted in his seat. Thankfully, they were now on Twenty-Third Street and Park, not far from Grace's women-only boarding house.

"How long have you worked at Mac & Arm's?" she asked.

"Since it opened five years ago."

"That must explain why you are able to work in various departments. I suppose you've met Mr. Armstrong."

"Of course," he said carefully, hiding his surprise.

"I just wondered. He's never out on the floor. I've never met him."

The back of his neck prickled. *Tell her. Tell her now.* Yet the words would not come. She would treat him differently. They always did. Could he not hold onto this one thing, this one rare opportunity, for a little longer?

You're selfish, Alex. You can still be her friend if she knows the truth.

No, he couldn't. That was impossible. He couldn't imagine being friends with a woman who was not his wife. Who was not Mary. He and his wife had shared a deep bond from years of shared knowledge, so close they could finish each other's sentences. Grace was an employee, nothing more.

He cleared his throat. "I know him well. Hard worker. Smart. Good with numbers."

"I hear he's a terror. That no secretary can tolerate him for long, and the staff are all petrified of him."

Alex didn't know what to say. His reputation, though unintentional, had been entirely earned. One or two incidents early on had sealed his fate. Gerald had forbidden Alex from roaming the store during hours of operation because he was afraid Alex would intimidate the employees or scare away the customers.

It had never bothered him before, but now he longed to change Grace's opinion of Mr. Armstrong. To prove he was a good person, honest and dedicated—not a terror.

"I don't know about *petrified*," he hedged. "And he's hardly a terror. That's just office gossip."

The carriage swung to the curb and slowed. "I'm certain you're right. You know how these things get started."

The carriage stopped. Grace uttered a cheerful good-bye and quickly stepped down to the walk. Alex didn't even get the chance to escort her to the door before she disappeared inside her residence.

The hack seemed eerily quiet on his way home. Normally he relished the silence to collect his thoughts. Tonight, however, he could only concentrate on what—or who—was missing.

Grace hurried inside, not even taking time to chat with the landlady before dashing up to her small room. She needed to be alone to contemplate what had transpired this evening.

Alex. There had been moments where he'd stared at her with such intensity, such longing... Had she imagined it? She certainly hadn't imagined him sniffing her hair during their brief embrace. Well, not an *embrace*, per se. More like he'd caught her to prevent her from falling on her face.

Goodness, he must think her a complete Clumsy Clara.

Grace removed her gloves and unpinned her hat. Her feet throbbed from standing in the window all night, and she yearned to peel off the layers of damp clothing.

How could she thank Alex for his assistance tonight? Perhaps she'd find him tomorrow and offer to buy him coffee.

Before she could undress, a knock sounded. For a brief second, she wondered if it could be Alex. *No, silly. He's not interested in you. He's still grieving his wife.*

Mrs. Hubert, her landlady, stood in the hall. "Hello, Mrs. Hubert."

"Hello, Grace." The older German woman was kind and considerate, sort of a second mother to the residents. She cared about the girls in her house, always asking questions and offering advice. She made certain they all ate properly and was not averse to offering her skill with a needle and thread, should the need arise. "I did not have a chance to speak with you when you came home."

"I apologize for that. It's been a long day and I'm exhausted."

"No problem, no problem. You girls these days, so busy." She smiled, her round face growing even rounder. "I am here to inquire about the rent. It was due yesterday, you know."

"Of course!" Grace's palms flew to her cheeks. "I am so sorry. How could I have forgotten? It's already the tenth of the month."

"You have been working very hard at the store, all those long hours. I was not worried, Grace. You're a good girl."

Yes, but mostly because she hadn't the money yet to explore the city's nightlife. Grace had been dying to visit the dance halls, like the Haymarket in the Tenderloin, ever since Helen, one of the other residents, had described the flashy costumes worn by the dancers on stage. The fancy outfits of the wealthy patrons were a sight to see as well, according to Helen.

Grace smiled at her landlady. "Thank you, Mrs. Hubert. Let me get you the money right away. Wait here." She hurried to the cigar box tucked high on a shelf in her closet. Pulling it down, she flipped open the top ...and froze.

The box contained less money than she remembered. A *lot* less money. Normally she just grabbed bills without looking. Obviously she'd lost track of the contents.

Biting her lip, she counted the paper money and coins. *Oh, no.* How had this happened? Living in New York City was expensive, certainly, and her wages at Mac & Arm's were meager at best. However, she hadn't spent extravagantly.

She earned six dollars and twenty-five cents each week working for Mr. Bernard, which covered her monthly rent. She'd brought thirty-three dollars from home for everything else. How much had she spent on food, streetcars, and the occasional treat? More than she'd thought, apparently.

Remember what they say about a fool and his money, her mother had warned her. *Budget yours carefully. You are on your own now.*

Her heart sank. Perhaps she could approach Mr. Bernard about a raise once the holiday windows were completed. Otherwise, she might need to find another job. Maybe two.

Swallowing her worry, Grace counted out twenty-five dollars for Mrs. Hubert. "Here you are." She handed the money to her landlady. "My apologies for not paying this sooner."

Mrs. Hubert slipped the bills into her apron. "Of course, my dear. I never worried for a moment. Not about you. You are one of the nice ones."

Grace had heard the occasional whisper about other girls, the ones who couldn't pay their rent. Those forced to explore more lucrative, less upstanding opportunities to earn money. Panic gathered in her throat, restricting her air as if her collar were buttoned too tightly. She didn't want to give up on her dreams and return to Farmington, where she'd most likely have to marry her one extremely unpleasant suitor, Horace Piles.

Grace Piles.

No, no, no. She would merely need to save more money. If she walked to the store instead of taking the streetcar and skipped lunch, she just might be able to afford her rent next month.

CHAPTER 4

The numbers in the ledger swam before Alex's eyes.

The house had long settled for the night while he'd attempted to work. His concentration had begun to wane, however. He'd spent the last hour trying not to think about Grace Shipley—and failing miserably.

Clumsy and innocent, Grace could not be more wrong for him. Yet, there was something about her, an effervescence that illuminated the space around her. She made things brighter. More interesting. Her laugh spread joy with the mere sound of it, the happy warmth burrowing in his veins. He didn't know how to defend himself against that.

Or the soft curves he'd encountered when he caught her falling off the ladder.

"A word, sir."

Alex glanced up to find Sarah's governess, Mrs. Beadle, frowning in the doorway. There was a determined set to her sturdy shoulders, one he recognized. She had come to take him to task. Sighing heavily, he rose. Whatever she had to say, he undoubtedly deserved it. "Of course. Would you care to sit?"

"No, thank you. I'll stand." A short, gray-haired woman, she

Miracle On Ladies' Mile

stepped closer and folded her hands. "Are you aware that tomorrow is Sarah's tenth birthday?"

"Of course. I had my staff wrap up a few things from the store—"

"I beg your pardon, sir, but I am well versed in how you handle your daughter's birthday. However, this year, merely sending generic presents from the store will not suffice."

"They're hardly generic. I spent at least five hundred dollars."

This did not appease Mrs. Beadle. In fact, it seemed to only irritate her further. "The money is not the point. The girl wants your time, sir. She wants to *know* you."

"That's ridiculous. She knows me. I'm her father."

"In the last six months, you have shared eight dinners and eleven breakfasts with your daughter. She is starved for affection. So starved that her only request for her tenth birthday is to spend the day with you. At the store."

Was Mrs. Beadle actually keeping track of how often he and Sarah dined? Regardless, those numbers were off. He'd spent more time with her than that... Hadn't he?

"I cannot bring her to the store with me. What would she do all day?"

Mrs. Beadle exhaled sharply and closed her eyes as if pained. "Sir, if I may be blunt. I know it is customary for children of a certain status to be reared independently of their parents. Therefore, I am not asking you to change your daily routine. However, for one day— on this *particular* day—allowances must be made."

The entire day? Alex swallowed hard. He loved Sarah with his entire being. If he had to give his life to spare hers, he would do it willingly. Gladly. But he did not know how to talk to her, this miniature version of his late wife. At least not yet. Right now, he couldn't look at Sarah without seeing Mary, without experiencing the shattering, soul-crushing loss of his wife.

"It is her tenth birthday," Mrs. Beadle added softly. "The late Mrs. Armstrong was very adamant that Sarah be included in all things. That she feels loved. I know the loss has been difficult for you, but

Sarah should not suffer in the face of your grief. Not on her birthday."

The urge to argue rose within him. He swiftly suppressed it. Mrs. Beadle had lived in the house since Sarah's birth, so any denials would fall on deaf ears. She'd seen and heard too much for that.

"This is what she has requested? To come to the store?"

"Yes. She wants to spend the day with you at the store."

How would sitting in his office, watching him pour over receipts and contracts, budgets and forecasts, possibly excite a ten-year-old girl? He often bored himself with the tedium of running a large accounting department. But there was no hope for it. Alex could not refuse Sarah this, even if he ended up heartsick by the end of the day.

He gave a curt nod. "Please have her ready to leave at half past six tomorrow morning."

Grace swirled the bright yellow paint with her brush. She was in the Mac & Arm's basement this morning, touching up the wooden ducklings for *The Ugly Duckling* window at Mr. Bernard's request. He and two assistants were instead working on dress alterations down the hall. Honestly, Grace would rather be working on the alterations. The paint smelled terrible.

After the windows are complete, then I can get back to sewing.

Merely thinking of the holiday windows caused giddiness to prickle over her skin. Would he return this evening? Silly to think he might. Alex must have a hundred more interesting things to do than to stand in those stuffy windows with her.

Still, a girl could dream.

When he'd caught her in his arms... Goodness, that was the stuff of novels where the romantic leading man saved the plucky heroine. Though one had to wonder why couldn't the plucky heroine save the hero every now and again? Men weren't infallible. They often needed rescuing, too.

Anyway, she hoped to see Alex again. He was nice. Helpful. Hand-

Miracle On Ladies' Mile 31

some. Not that she had aspirations about the man. That wasn't it at all. She'd only been in New York City a few weeks and, as much as she loved it here, friends were hard to come by. She sensed he could use one as well, now that his wife had died. He'd sounded so sad when talking about her.

A noise caught her attention. She assumed it was Mr. Bernard or one of the other employees until a quiet voice asked, "What are you doing?"

Grace's head snapped up. A young girl stood not far away, her attention on Grace's ducklings. What on earth was she doing down here? Had a customer's child wandered away from the store? Seeing no parent or adult behind the child, she said, "Hello. I'm finishing the paint on these ducklings."

The girl stepped closer. She had a mop of messy blond curls and clear blue eyes, set off nicely by the china blue dress she wore. White ribbons adorned the neckline and sleeves, which perfectly matched the ribbon on her head. Grace admired the crafting of the dress. The cut, stitching, and fabric proclaimed it an expensive garment.

"Why?"

Grace set the brush in the paint so it didn't dry out. "Did you see those windows on the outside of the store, the ones with brown paper covering them?" The girl nodded. "Those are our special holiday windows. You cannot tell anyone but each window shall be a different fairy tale. Have you ever read *The Ugly Duckling*?"

"Oh, yes. That's one of my favorites. I love when the duckling turns into the swan."

"Me too," Grace said and pointed across the room. "See the swan over there? I painted it yesterday."

The girl followed Grace's finger and then gasped at the large, ornate swan. "He's beautiful. That must have taken a long time."

It certainly had. "What's your name?"

"Sarah."

"Nice to meet you, Sarah. I'm Grace."

Sarah bobbed a curtsy. "Nice to meet you, too. May I help you paint?"

Grace eyed the expensive dress one more time. "Are you shopping in the store with your mother?"

"I don't have a mother. I'm here with my father. But he's working upstairs."

"Oh." Was her father one of the clerks? Or perhaps one of the supervisors or accountants from the top floor of the building. "Won't he be worried about you?"

"No. He told me to go explore the store."

Go explore the store? Alone? Grace's lips tightened. What sort of father turned his young daughter loose in Mac & Arm's? Was he unaware of the dangers of New York City? Heavens, her family was worried sick about her being away from the rest of them in Pennsylvania—and she was nineteen. They insisted on hearing from her twice a week, either by telephone or letter. If she didn't write or call, she imagined her relatives would storm Ladies' Mile looking for her.

The last thing she wanted to do was tell Sarah to leave. At least here, Grace could keep an eye on the girl and ensure she was well cared for. Some lunatic might very well drag a young girl off if there were no one around to protect her. And there was definitely enough work to keep them both busy all day. "Well, I'd be happy for the help. There's a lot to finish and I'm all by myself today."

Rising, Grace untied the apron she wore to protect her dress. "I don't have another cover, so you'll have to use mine. We can't have you getting paint on that pretty dress. Here, hold up your arms."

"I don't care if this dress gets ruined. It makes me look like a baby. I keep telling my governess that I want a lady's dress. One like yours."

Grace wrapped Sarah in the apron then moved behind her to tie the strings. "How old are you?"

"I'm ten. Today's my birthday."

"My goodness! Happy birthday." The girl's father had brought her to the store and turned her out by herself on her *birthday*? Goodness, Sarah's father sounded perfectly awful.

Grace's tenth birthday had been celebrated with a big family picnic on a nearby lake. There had been swimming and sack races. Pie and horseback rides. Her father had carried her on his back almost the whole day. The memory not only caused her to miss her father terribly, it had her heart aching for everything Sarah seemed to lack in a paternal figure.

"Don't you agree that ten is old enough for a proper lady's dress?"

Grace decided not to lie, even if it was the girl's birthday. "No, I don't. You still need to wait a few more years."

Sarah's face fell. "I hate these ribbons. I can't wait to be older and wear something like your dress. It's quite pretty."

"Thank you." Grace had designed this one based on a dress in last year's Sears catalog. It was a two-piece ensemble of heavy amethyst-colored cotton, long sleeved, with a vertical pattern of light green bows imprinted into the fabric. The bodice had a lace overlay with a single ruffle. "I made it myself."

"You did?" Sarah's eyes went huge. "You are very talented. Do you also design the dresses for Mac & Arm's?"

I wish. "No, I've only been working here about a month. I'm still the new girl. Someday, though, I hope to design dresses for the store."

"Well, you should. I would wear your dresses."

Grace laughed, warmed by the compliment. It was nice to have a supporter, even if she was only ten. "Shall we get to painting?"

CHAPTER 5

Grace put down her paintbrush. "Now, all our ducklings are done."

Sarah had already finished her wooden bird, so she leaned over to inspect Grace's work. "That looks nice. Will these go in the window tonight?"

"No. Tonight I am finishing the *Snow Queen* window. Want to see the pieces?"

"Yes!" Sarah said quickly and began pushing her chair away from the wooden workbench.

Laughing, Grace rose. "Let's clean up first and get you out of that apron."

Once they had cleaned the brushes and set the painted pieces on the floor to dry, Grace led the girl to the rear of the workshop where the completed props were stored. A large snow queen doll, with long, ice blue hair and a silver gown, rested flat on the table. A silver and blue sleigh waited to be placed on the faux ice on the window's floor.

"She's beautiful," Sarah whispered, reaching out to touch the doll's hair. "I love her dress."

"Thank you." The dress had taken quite a long time and the silver fabric had been hard and unforgiving. Grace was quite proud of the result. Based on a Renaissance-era design, the gown had long sleeves

Miracle On Ladies' Mile   35

trimmed with white fur, a basque waistline dropping into layers of diaphanous silk, and a high Queen Elizabeth-style collar around the neckline.

"You sewed this?" Sarah fingered the seed pearls on the bodice.

"I did. It wasn't easy."

"Can you make me one?" When Grace didn't answer right away, Sarah turned wide, pleading eyes to her. "Oh please, Grace? *Please?*"

"I don't know. This took a long time." It would also cost money she didn't have, unless Sarah's father paid for it. She eyed the doll and the girl, who actually seemed about the same size. "Hmm. Let's measure you. If I'm correct, it's possible you could have this dress with only a few minor alterations. Then we can ask Mr. Bernard if he'd be willing to part with it after the holidays."

Sarah clapped happily as Grace went to fetch the tape. In a few minutes, they had Grace's measurements. "I'll likely need to let out the bodice to accommodate a corset." Grace set her pad and measuring tape on the counter. "The doll doesn't have on any undergarments," she whispered to the little girl, and Sarah giggled.

"Thank you. Papa will just *have* to take me to a party if I wear this dress."

"You might be a smidgen young for parties. But perhaps you could wear this when he takes you for ice cream. Or riding in Central Park."

Sarah's face fell. "He never takes me those places."

"No?" Grace was surprised. What did fathers do with their daughters in New York City?

"He's very busy." Sarah's voice was flat, as if she were repeating what had been droned into her head. "My governess takes me out sometimes, though."

Sometimes? The tips of Grace's ears turned hot. Undoubtedly, her skin had gone scarlet with outrage on Sarah's behalf. No father should be too busy for his child. Before he'd passed on, Grace's father had run a successful farm, but he'd always made time for Grace and her siblings. They'd never felt unloved or unwanted.

Grace took a deep breath. Perhaps the situation wasn't as terrible as she'd assumed. "He must prefer to play games with you and your siblings indoors."

Sarah shook her head. "No, and I don't have any brothers or sisters. It's just me."

"Does he read to you? Draw pictures with you?"

"No, but my governess will sometimes do those things."

"So when do you see your father?"

"If Papa is home, we have dinner together."

If he is home. Grace clenched her fists, tamping down a few choice words for the man raising Sarah. This was unacceptable. Disgraceful. Children from wealthy families were often sent to boarding schools away from their parents. However, Sarah lived at home. He ignored this wonderful child right under his nose. How could he?

Grace would give anything to have had more time with her own father. Just one more minute to tell him all those things she'd never been able to say.

Egregious, this man's treatment of his daughter. Someone should knock some sense into him.

"Grace, are you all right? You're tearing your apron."

She glanced down and saw the cloth disintegrating in her tight fists. "Sarah, I'm taking you upstairs. Let's go see your father. Where exactly does he work?"

"Up on the top floor. In the office next to Mr. McCall."

Grace paused. "So that means your father is...Mr. Armstrong?"

"Yes. Do you know him?"

Pieces fell into place, upsetting Grace even further. She threw the crumpled apron on the table, and the cloth thumped on the wood. Everything she'd heard about Armstrong was true—and then some. No wonder the staff never saw him. The man couldn't even be bothered to interact with his own daughter.

She was so angry the back of her teeth ached. Still, reprimanding Sarah's father was out of the question now, not if Grace wanted to keep her job. And, unfortunately, she needed this job. Desperately. Perhaps she would try a few polite suggestions. Respectfully advise

Mr. Armstrong on how to be a better father. Because obviously, the man hadn't a clue.

Clasping Sarah's hand, Grace led the girl to the stairs. Inside the store, workers were decorating for Christmas, with every column being swathed in gold, silver, and red. Long strings of red satin ribbon would soon drape the ceiling, gathering in the center under a massive chandelier. A stately Christmas tree, its branches wrapped in electric lights, had been placed under the large light fixture. She'd overheard Mr. Bernard saying a tree just like it had been placed in the White House for President Cleveland and the First Lady.

When she and Sarah reached the third floor, a loud voice rang out. "Sarah?"

They turned to find Mr. McCall striding toward them, a grin on his face. Three men carrying notebooks trailed the store co-owner. "Hello, Miss Shipley. I see you've met Sarah."

Mr. McCall held out his hand and Grace shook it. "Hello, Mr. McCall. Nice to see you again. Sarah and I have been having fun down in the design studio."

"I've been painting ducks," Sarah proclaimed proudly. "I did a good job. Didn't I, Grace?"

Grace placed a fond hand on the girl's head. "Indeed, you did. You're welcome to help me any time you'd like."

The girl's eyes grew wide. "Truly? Any time?"

"Of course." She looked up at Mr. McCall. "I was just returning Sarah to her father. I wouldn't want Mr. Armstrong to worry over her."

"That was considerate of you. I'm certain he'd appreciate that. Why don't I take Sarah upstairs for you?"

Grace tried to mask her disappointment. She couldn't very well argue with Mr. McCall over this. Mac & Arm's was his store, after all.

Dang it.

"If it's no trouble," she hedged. "Otherwise, I'm more than happy—"

"No trouble at all. Is it, shortcake?" He reached behind Sarah's ear and pulled a quarter out with his fingers. "Look what I found!"

Sarah did not appear impressed. "Mr. McCall, I'm ten now. I know that's just a trick."

Mr. McCall winked. "I'll have to work on some new ones then, see if I can't fool you next time. Come along. Let's take you back to your father's office."

Sarah turned to Grace. "Thank you for allowing me to stay with you. May I really come back?"

"Anytime you'd like," Grace answered, meaning every word. "I hope to see you again."

Gerald strolled into the office, holding hands with a beautiful blond child. "Look who I found."

Alex paused in his calculations and looked up. His chest compressed at the sight of his daughter, the memory of his wife so vivid it physically hurt. He fought to push down the pain, to keep it locked in the small compartment inside his heart that belonged to no one else other than Mary.

He rose and smiled at the two of them. At least, he tried to smile. Judging by the expression on Gerald's face, Alex failed miserably.

He thrust his hands into his pockets. "Did you have fun exploring the store, sweetheart? I expected to see you carrying at least a few packages. Did you not see anything you wanted?"

She shrugged. "The store is so big. I couldn't find the toys, so I just kept riding the escalator down."

The basement, Gerald mouthed. "One of the nice designers brought you upstairs, didn't she?" Gerald said to Sarah. "Something about painting ducks."

She, he'd said. Had it been Grace? Alex's skin burned with awareness, an interest he immediately quashed. He glanced at his partner. "Thank you, Gerald."

The other man nodded and reached to lay a hand on Sarah's shoulder. "Enjoy the rest of the day, Princess Sarah. Come and say good-bye before you go home, all right?"

Miracle On Ladies' Mile

"I will," Sarah said. "Thank you, Mr. McCall."

Gerald shut the office door. Alex lowered to his haunches until he and Sarah were eye-to-eye. "Were you painting?"

"I was, Papa. You would not believe all the wonderful things in the basement. There were ducks and swans and snow queens. And Grace said I could have the Snow Queen's dress!"

So it had been Grace. Shocked, Alex tried to wipe all traces of emotion from his face. Had Grace learned Sarah was his daughter? What had the two of them discussed?

"You have to let me come back tomorrow," his daughter was saying, regaining his attention.

"Tomorrow?" He pulled back in surprise. "I cannot bring you here every day."

Her thin blond brows lowered. "Why not? I've been very quiet. Mrs. Beadle said if I was good you might let me visit the store again."

"Yes, but not right away. You have lessons and...things. Studies. Sitting in my office every day would be very boring."

"But I won't be in your office. I'll go to the basement and help Grace. She said I could." Sarah thrust her chin out, a reminder of his wife's very stubborn personality. God help them all if Sarah inherited that trait.

He tried for calm and rational. "Grace is an employee at the store. She has work to do. It will not help if you are constantly in her way."

"I won't be in her way. I can paint and draw. Help her design clothing."

"Clothing?" Hadn't Grace been hired to merely work on the holiday windows? Yes, she sewed her own clothing but that was a far cry from designing for Mac & Arm's. As far as Alex knew, she'd be out of a job by New Year's.

"Yes, she sews all her own clothes. She made the most beautiful dress for the Snow Queen. Don't you know her?"

Yes, he knew Grace. Knew how she rolled her lip between her teeth when she concentrated. How her blue eyes sparkled when she was excited. Knew of her tempting curves and inviting smile. But he'd purposely refrained from telling her his name. Had Sarah informed her instead?

"I'm not certain. Did she tell you that we'd met?"

"No, but I told her you worked upstairs."

Relief cascaded through him, quickly followed by guilt. He dragged a hand through his hair and let out a long breath. Deceiving someone about his identity should not have pleased him this much.

"Please, Papa? May I come to work with you tomorrow?"

"Absolutely not." He straightened and smoothed the fabric of his trousers. "I allowed you to accompany me today because it's your birthday. But tomorrow, you must return to your lessons with Mrs. Beadle."

"But, please—"

"No," he said, stronger this time. "I cannot have you disturbing the employees, Sarah. This is a place of business, not a boarding school." He spun on his heel and strode to his desk. He was being harsh but she had to understand. With her around, anywhere in the store, he'd constantly be on edge. Besides, she should be studying and practicing at home, not getting underfoot here.

He stood behind the massive, ornate desk and shuffled a few papers resting on top. There were one or two more things that needed his attention before lunch. "Now, where shall we eat to celebrate your birthday? There is an ice cream shop two blocks away. How about we give it a try?"

"I want to go home."

Alex's gaze flew toward his daughter. Her bottom lip was quivering, her small body stiff, fists clenched at her sides. He dropped the papers in his hands and tried to gentle his tone. "Home? But we still have a few more hours left of your birthday. Why would you want to return home early?"

She didn't say anything, so Alex came around the desk. Sarah's eyes were glassy as if she might cry. Dear God, he hoped not. Mrs. Beadle was better equipped to handle tears over him. "Sarah, answer me."

"I-I'd just rather return home, is all."

Miracle On Ladies' Mile

He inwardly winced, his incompetence as a father both frustrating and embarrassing. He should have known this would be a disaster, that he would cause her unhappiness. He had no idea how to relate to Sarah. No longer a child and not yet a woman, his daughter was a dashed mystery. Now her birthday had been ruined.

At times like this, he truly missed Mary. *You would know what to say. You would make everything all right again.*

Loss rippled through his chest, the pain echoing like a stone thrown into a deep well. He opened his mouth to argue with Sarah. To reason with her. But what could he say? He couldn't change his mind and allow her to dog him to the store every day. Perhaps he could ask Mrs. Beadle to explain it to her. Surely the governess would be able to put it in terms Sarah could better understand. Alex would invariably fail at getting his point across.

He sighed and accepted defeat. "If you're certain, I will escort you home."

"I'm certain—and there's no need for you to leave the store." Dry, determined eyes full of weariness looked up at him. "I'm old enough that our driver may see me safely home."

He hated how grown up and sad she sounded just then. God willing, Mrs. Beadle could fix this. "That may be true," he told her. "But I still plan to do it regardless."

CHAPTER 6

Grace had nearly finished the Snow Queen window when Alex stepped into the rear of the display. The first thing she noticed were the dark circles under his eyes and the grim set to his mouth. "Hello," she said with a small smile.

Even though he appeared exhausted, she was happy to see him. Part of her had hoped he'd join her again this evening, and now he was here, wearing a navy suit with a green and blue striped silk vest. His dark hair had been oiled today, a severe style that showed off his strong eyebrows and angular jaw. So roughly handsome, he bordered on pretty. Her heart thumped hard, excitement filling her chest to near bursting.

"Good evening, Grace." He slumped against the wall. His gaze swept the display she'd been toiling on. "Nice work. This is quite beautiful."

"Thank you." Snow covered the floor, a large white sparkly sled on top. The Snow Queen stood to the side, her long silver and blue dress floating around her. An electric fan would blow the snow around inside the window once she finished. "You look as if you've had a trying day."

"It has been unusually difficult."

"That's a shame. In which department were you working today?"

"Children."

No wonder the poor man appeared so harried. "They can be trying."

"So I've learned. I confess I never know what to say or do around them."

"With my siblings and cousins, little ones were constantly underfoot at home."

"How did you stay sane?"

"I listened to them. Most children merely want to know someone is interested in what they have to say."

He nodded slowly, as if absorbing this bit of wisdom. "What if they don't want to talk?"

"All children want to talk. They are born seeking attention from others, especially elders. A young girl showed up in the basement today, in fact." Grace refrained from saying whose daughter. No need to disparage Sarah or Mr. Armstrong in front of another Mac & Arm's staff member. "One of the employee's children. I could hardly get a word in edgewise."

"Is that so?" Alex straightened off the wall and thrust his hands in his trouser pockets. "What did she say, exactly?"

"Well, I don't know if I could say *exactly*—"

"In general. What sort of things did you discuss?"

She began to unfurl the painted winter background that would complete the display. Alex came to assist her, taking the opposite edge of the canvas and separating the two sides. "We talked about art, mostly. She loves to draw and create things, so she was very interested in what we do at Mac & Arm's. Here, get the ladder and you can hang this on the hooks for me."

Alex settled the ladder into place and climbed up. He reached for the canvas. They worked easily, comfortably, as Grace held the canvas and Alex secured it into place. "It was very kind of you to entertain her," he said. "Why was she wandering the store?"

"Bored. Her father is an employee. She was just exploring, as young girls like to do."

"They do?"

"Of course. Didn't you like to explore as a child?"

"Yes, but I was a boy."

Obviously, she wanted to say. "Girls are no different from boys. Not at that age, at least."

He made a sound of surprise in his throat as he stepped down to move the ladder to the right. She grinned to herself. Clearly, Alex had no children of his own. They worked in silence until the canvas was complete. Grace dusted off her hands and beamed. "Another window finished. That's three. I may need to complete two tomorrow, otherwise I won't meet the deadline."

"You shouldn't have to do these all by yourself. I'm still uncertain why no one is helping you."

"Everyone else is busy with alterations this week. The ladies have all just ordered their dresses for Christmas parties, and Mr. Bernard is overwhelmed."

"Then he should hire more staff," Alex grumbled. "You should not be here alone each night."

"But I'm not alone. I have you." She tried for a flippant, casual tone but the words were a husky rasp. He caught her gaze and held it, his dark eyes unreadable in the low overhead light. She could feel her skin heat as a flush swept over her, yet she did not look away. She couldn't, not when he stared at her so sharply, with his jaw clamped tight.

What was he thinking about? Could have been a variety of things, like his day. What he wanted for dinner. Christmas presents he needed to buy. Yet something told her it wasn't any of those things. Call it feminine intuition, but she knew he was thinking about her. Kissing her, perhaps? She licked her lips, wetting them, and wondered what it would feel like.

Then Alex's lids closed, his gaze shuttering to break the moment. Ignoring the disappointment winding through her, she busied herself with cleaning up the unnecessary pieces in the window.

"A lot of good I did you," Alex finally said. "The window was mostly finished by the time I arrived."

"True, but I will never turn down a man willing to climb on a ladder."

"I'll also stow the ladder."

"My hero," she said on an exaggerated sigh.

He chuckled, a rare and glorious sound indeed. "And I insist on driving you home again tonight."

A shiver raced down Grace's spine at the thought of sharing another intimate carriage ride with Alex. There was something happening between the two of them, a spark that merely needed the right conditions to catch and burn. Would he have returned this evening if he wasn't interested in her? She doubted it. The notion gave her hope.

"Thank you, I'd like that. But only if it's not any trouble for you."

"You're worth the trouble, Grace."

Happiness bubbled up in her chest. Yes, definitely interested.

Things had changed between them.

Alex didn't know what, exactly, but Grace made no effort to keep a respectable distance in the carriage. In fact, she sat fairly snug against him. Shoulders touching, her thigh molded to the outside of his. He felt himself drowning in an ocean of longing and desire as warm, sweet-smelling woman assaulted his senses.

What are you doing? He closed his eyes briefly and forced the fanciful musings away. Despite her freckles, radiance, and bottomless cheerfulness, she was an innocent woman. One he had no practical use for.

Truth be told, he enjoyed the way she stared at him, with a genuine interest not based on his bank account or position, but as a man. She lacked any artifice whatsoever, wearing both her ambition and her heart on her sleeve. He liked that about her. He also liked her infectious laugh.

Clever and funny, this young woman drew him to her. She was a bright and dazzling lure on a hook, Alex the hapless fish.

But, he'd been ensnared before and the results had nearly destroyed him. He couldn't risk allowing that to happen once more. Steeling his spine, he shifted and put distance between them.

The movement seemed to jar her out of her reverie. She said, "This is silly. I have no idea where you live. Is this terribly out of your way?"

"No, it's not out of my way." A lie, considering he lived some thirty blocks to the north on Fifth Avenue.

"Thank goodness. I already feel guilty enough about not contributing to the fare."

Alex didn't care about the fare. Offering to drive her had been a momentary madness, a way to prevent her from taking a late street-car. He didn't care for the idea of her standing out in the cold, waiting, and then traveling with a bunch of strangers where any manner of terrible things could transpire.

And if he'd stayed later at his desk than necessary in order to come visit the windows, well...he was merely being a good friend.

Are you seriously lying to yourself?

He shrugged off that inner voice. There would be plenty of time for self-reflection at home with a stiff drink in his hand.

"I need to save every penny I can," Grace continued. "I had no idea New York City would be so expensive."

Yes, how well he remembered. He and Mary had worried and scrimped when they first moved to the city. He'd quickly landed the job with Gerald, starting out at what seemed a princely sum of eleven dollars a week. With a meal of potatoes for months, he and Mary saved every coin they could in anticipation of starting a family and moving into better quarters. Bittersweet melancholy swelled in his throat.

He forced himself back to the present. "Have you asked Mr. Bernard for a raise?"

"No, not yet. Why? Do you think I should?"

"Absolutely, considering the number of hours you've been putting in. You deserve to be fairly compensated for your efforts."

"Perhaps I will. I was so happy to get the job at Mac & Arm's. As I'm sure you know, they pay higher wages than most of the other department stores."

Yes, they did. Alex and Gerald insisted on it. Both of them had been raised with very little and recalled the hardship of surviving on a meager weekly salary. They kept the wages at Mac & Arm's above the usual hourly rates, which helped in not only attracting the best staff, but also retaining them. "I had heard that."

"Even still, six dollars and twenty-five cents a week doesn't go very far here."

He snapped to attention. "Six dollars and twenty-five cents? That's ludicrous. You should be making—" He bit off the words. How would a lowly sales clerk know the salaries in every Mac & Arm's department?

But Alex knew because he headed up the finances. Grace should be earning at least eight dollars a week in the design department, even as a new assistant. That meant Bernard had hired her at a much lower salary than everyone else. Why? Because she was a woman? Plenty of women worked at Mac & Arm's, though the other assistant designers were male. He would have a very long discussion with Bernard tomorrow.

"I should be making, what? Do you know someone new in the design department who earns more than I do?"

Yes, only everybody.

He shrugged, attempting to relax. "I was just going to say you should be making enough to live on."

"That would certainly be nice." She chewed her lip, and her gloved fingers knotted in her lap. "Why are you being so kind to me?"

His hands flexed, muscles working as he tried to think of an answer. Only, he couldn't. There was no good reason for continuing to stay late and help her. "Maybe you look as if you need a friend."

"I suppose that's true." She huffed a laugh. "There are a few girls in the boarding house with whom I'm friendly. We often go out on our days off. Otherwise, I'm at the store."

"That doesn't sound like much fun." Alex didn't know a lot about young women, except for Mary, and his wife had been very social. They'd hosted small dinner parties, gone to the theater, walked to explore in the city together... He'd often teased her, saying she couldn't sit still if someone had paid her.

"I suppose my life's a rather dull existence, but it won't be forever. What about you? What do you like to do for fun?"

He opened his mouth, but nothing came out. It had been years since he'd engaged in any activity deemed "fun." He waved his hand. "I've been working hard recently."

She nodded as if she'd expected this answer. "Helen, a girl in my boarding house, knows I want to design clothing. She says I must find time to visit the Haymarket to see the costumes."

Alex frowned. The Tenderloin district's crown jewel of sin, the Haymarket was a brothel lightly masquerading as a dance hall. The social set liked the bawdiness of it, while the criminal element liked the opportunities for vice within. "The Haymarket is full of...degenerates. Drunks and unscrupulous ladies."

"It cannot be so bad if Helen has been there. I hear even the society ladies frequent it. Besides, I want to see the dancing. I hear ladies do the can-can on stage."

Yes, they did. With extra-wide slits in their drawers, leaving nothing to the imagination. Alex shifted to face Grace. "Promise me you won't go with your friend. That neighborhood is dangerous, especially at night. You should have a proper escort."

"But I don't have any male friends willing to serve as an escort."

"I *am* your friend and a man, which is why I'm advising you not to go."

Her shoulders slumped, but only for a moment. She instantly perked up. "What if—"

She bit off what she'd been about to say, so he prompted, "What?"

"No, it's silly. I just thought maybe...well, maybe you'd like to go."

"Go where?"

"To the Haymarket. With me." She waited a beat but when he didn't respond, she said, "See? Silly. Forget it."

Miracle On Ladies' Mile

"It's silly for you to consider going there, no matter who escorts you. It's not a fitting outing for a woman like you."

"*A woman like me?*"

He didn't like the shrill way she repeated it, incredulously, as if she weren't a fresh-faced innocent. "Come now. You know what I mean. You're from Pennsylvania. You have freckles on your nose."

She stiffened, her eyes narrowing. "I am not a rube, Alex. I may be young but I have a job. I live in a boarding house on my own. I take care of myself. And I'm sorry if you don't like my freckles. I realize freckles are bourgeois to the fancier set, but mine are the result of a life well lived with my family in *Pennsylvania*. I won't apologize for them."

"I never said—"

"And furthermore, I no longer invite you to escort me to the Haymarket. *A woman like me* shall instead ask one of the young men working in the design department to take me. They all seem friendly enough."

He jerked. The words sliced through him like a pair of blunt scissors. No. Just...no. Grace and some over-eager, randy puppy? At a dance hall with more dark corners than chairs? Absolutely not. Alex would never allow that. "Do not ask one of the men you work with. I'll take you." He'd likely go straight to hell for corrupting her, but at least she would be safe.

She sat back in the seat and fixed her gaze out the window. "Too late. The invitation has been rescinded."

He was bungling this, badly. He'd hurt her feelings, just as he'd hurt Sarah's earlier. At least he could reason with Grace, perhaps offer a logical apology to smooth things over. "Grace, please. I'm sorry. I never meant to imply that you're lacking in any way. I think you're quite clever, in fact."

She glanced at him over her shoulder. "You do?"

"I do. I also think you're talented, funny, and kind."

She gave him a brilliant smile, one he felt down to his toes. "The invitation has been reissued."

They were back to this?

"And before you think of reneging, you've already agreed to take me."

He silently cursed. "I have no one to blame but myself for allowing you to manipulate me into this, do I?"

"I did no such thing. Now, how is tomorrow night for you?"

Terrible, but he'd keep his word—even if it killed him. They should take his carriage, in case they needed a quick exit. Like if Grace fainted as a result of the debauchery she would undoubtedly witness. "Fine. We'll go after work. Not too late, though."

The carriage slowed as her face brightened, eyes gleaming as if he had offered her the moon. She touched his hand, the lightest brush of her gloved fingers against his skin. "Thank you, Alex." Before he could react, she threw open the latch and climbed out the carriage door.

He looked down at where she'd touched his hand and a thick, slow heat wound through his blood. A simple touch and he was tingling all over, as if he'd never had a woman caress him before. Grace continued to surprise him. Would she be as adventurous in bed?

Christ, where had that come from? He should not contemplate such things, not with a woman like her.

The phrase caused him to smile. He hadn't meant to offend her. What he'd been trying to say was that she was not like other women. She was innocent, unsullied by this rough and dangerous city. Still trusting and kind. Hell, if she weren't a virgin he'd be shocked.

And she would remain a virgin, no matter his fantasies of late. No matter how many times he'd brought himself off to thoughts of tasting her mouth, her nipples. Dreaming of the sweetness between her legs. How tight and hot she would be around him. Her whimpers when she came—

A shudder went through him, and he forced himself to think of boring things. Ledgers and profit margins. Getting his shoes shined. A political rally. He could not lust after her like this. It was unseemly at his age. Besides, he had no intention of entering a relationship again, let alone a marriage, and anything that implied otherwise would only mislead her. She was no wealthy widow or seasoned flirt, and he was no longer a seventeen-year-old boy. He knew better.

He exhaled. Tomorrow night was going to be utter torture.

CHAPTER 7

I never meant to imply that you're lacking in any way. I think you're quite clever.

Grace floated through her work in the basement the next morning, still giddy over last night's encounter with Alex. There was more than just friendship between them—at least she was beginning to hope as much. He made her feel so alive, so full of energy, and she thought he'd started to smile a bit more in her presence, no longer the dour man from the night they met.

Keep your feet firmly on the ground, her mother's voice warned in Grace's head. Fair enough, she was probably getting ahead of herself. However, it was her first outing in the biggest city in America—and to the Haymarket with Alex, no less. Wasn't she allowed a little fanciful dreaming?

Indeed, if a girl conjured up the perfect evening with the perfect man, this would be it. So she would concentrate on tonight and not worry about the future. Nor would she look for hidden meaning in his every word and glance. She'd act sophisticated and worldly, not like a freckle-faced girl from Pennsylvania.

And if she tripped again and he had to catch her...well, then she'd do her best to enjoy the gentle cradle of his arms and the strong wall of his chest in that one moment.

Miracle On Ladies' Mile

Grinning at her foolish thoughts, she filled her arms with as many ducklings as she could manage and hurried toward the basement stairs. A small figure darted into her path, startling her.

"Hello, Grace!"

"Sarah. Goodness, you gave me a scare." An older woman hovered nearby. A relative or governess? "Hello to you both."

"Good morning, Miss Grace," the woman said. "I pardon the disruption. I am Sarah's governess, Mrs. Beadle. Sarah insisted on returning to Mac & Arm's in order to assist you. She said the two of you discussed this at length yesterday."

At length? Grace shot Sarah a knowing look. *The little scamp.* She'd wanted to escape to the store today and had used Grace to do it. Still, she didn't have the heart to turn the girl away. "I'd be glad for her help, if it's not a problem for you." Lord knew the girl's father wouldn't mind. From what Sarah had said, he was anxious to wash his hands of his daughter.

"Yes, that would be fine. Her father has agreed to the occasional visit. Correct, Sarah?"

Sarah nodded eagerly—a little too eagerly. "Yes, he did. Thank you very much, Mrs. Beadle."

"I have two windows to design today," Grace told them, "so I'll take Sarah upstairs with me most of the day. Would you care to wait here, Mrs. Beadle, or perhaps the café on the second floor?"

"If you don't mind, I will visit my sister. She lives a few blocks away. What time shall I return to collect Sarah?"

"Let's say four o'clock. In plenty of time to get washed up for supper, right?"

"Yes, I should say so. Sarah, mind Miss Grace and I'll see you this afternoon. And please, try not to bother your father at work. He's a very busy man, and he won't appreciate distractions."

Grace clamped her lips shut, pressing hard to prevent herself from inserting any unwarranted (but entirely justified, in her opinion) comments about the girl's father. Children were not distractions. When she decided to have her own children, she would certainly never treat them as if they were a bother.

"Yes, Mrs. Beadle," Sarah replied dutifully.

With a final nod, Mrs. Beadle disappeared toward the stairs. Grace smirked knowingly at Sarah. "You have a promising future as a confidence man, little lady."

Sarah's cheeks flushed and she looked down to study her shoes. "You said I could come back to help any time."

"So I did. But did your father agree as well?"

"Maybe."

Grace rolled her eyes. No use arguing over it now. "Fine, but if I get discharged for aiding and abetting it's on your head. Grab the rest of those ducklings off that counter over there, will you? We'll take them up to the window."

The girl practically skipped to the counter. She collected the ducklings and followed Grace up the stairs into the store. The two of them quickly navigated the crowds to reach the holiday windows. Grace pulled the door open, allowing Sarah to enter before she followed.

"It's so dark in here," Sarah whispered as the door closed behind them. Only a sliver of daylight showed around the edges of the brown paper.

"Hold on." Grace put her ducks down and pulled the chain to turn on the electric bulb on the ceiling. Light flooded the cluttered space. "There. Now we can see what we're doing."

"What will you do first?" Sarah asked.

"Well, *we* are going to set up our pond. First, we'll put down the dyed cotton as our dirt, then the palm fronds all around the edges."

"Will the pond have real water in it?"

"No. I've learned that lesson already. I am using glass, and we'll put blue textured paper beneath it."

Sarah appeared enthralled at this simple design trick. "You are so clever, Grace."

Alex had said the same last night, the memory causing giddiness to break out over her skin. *Just a few hours, Grace.* A few hours and they'd be off to the Haymarket for a night of fun...and perhaps more.

She pushed all those thoughts aside for now and focused on her task. "Thank you. Now, the first rule of design is that you cannot be afraid to fail. I actually fell into a pool of real water in another window. Nearly ruined my boots. Hence the glass. Are you ready to get started?"

"Yes, please!"

Alex ground his teeth together as he studied the numbers. One of the Mac & Arm's perfume suppliers had tried to cheat the store out of nearly one hundred bottles. His accountants had caught the mistake and brought it to Alex's attention. Alex hated when things didn't add up.

Circling the figures, he jotted a terse note for the perfumers. A knock sounded. "Yes?"

His current secretary appeared. Alex hadn't yet memorized her name. Miss Roger? Miss Rotter?

"Sir, Mr. Bernard is here to see you."

Excellent. Alex leaned back in his chair. "Send him in, please, Miss…"

"Roberts, sir."

"Yes, thank you. Will you ask Mr. McCall to join us as well?" Gerald liked to be involved when Alex reprimanded employees, since Gerald excelled at smoothing over ruffled feathers in a way Alex had never been able to manage.

She nodded and disappeared. Seconds later, the head designer for Mac & Arm's came in. Well dressed and smartly put together, Mr. Bernard carried himself with an air of importance. He appeared more annoyed than intimidated at a summons to the co-owner's office.

"Good afternoon, Mr. Bernard. Please, have a seat." Alex gestured to one of the two chairs in front of his desk. "Mr. McCall will be joining us as well."

"It is my hope this will not take long." Mr. Bernard sniffed as he lowered himself into a chair. "We are *très occupé* with the Christmas orders."

"Yes, I realize. I wanted to speak with you about—"

The door burst open and Gerald hurried in. He shut the wood panel behind him and crossed to the empty chair. "Nice to see you, Felix." He shook the designer's hand. "Have we started?"

"No, just beginning." Alex put his elbows on the chair rests and steepled his fingers. "Mr. Bernard, how much do you pay your associate designers?"

Mr. Bernard blinked, his pointed mustache twitching. "Eight dollars a week, as is the standard."

"Then perhaps you could tell me why there is an associate designer only making six dollars and twenty-five cents a week?"

Bernard's eyes darted away as he shifted in the seat. "*Non,* that cannot be correct."

"Oh, but it is. Miss Shipley has been earning significantly less than everyone else since she was hired more than a month ago. Can you explain that?"

"I cannot." Bernard gave a nervous laugh and held up his hands. "This must be some sort of accounting error."

No two words in the English language grated on Alex's nerves quite like *accounting error.*

He leaned in, his voice low and hard. "I assure you, my accounting department has made no error. They were told to pay her six-twenty-five and that is what she has been receiving."

"Now, I'm certain there's a reasonable explanation here," Gerald said calmly. "Perhaps you were mistaken about the hiring salary, Felix. Or were you starting her at a lower salary as a trial?"

"Or maybe you thought, as a young girl, Miss Shipley wouldn't know the difference," Alex growled.

"No, yes! A trial. *Oui!*" Bernard snapped his fingers. "I wanted the girl to prove herself before I promoted her to associate designer."

"That is not our policy," Alex said. "While other department stores may play fast and loose with salaries, we do not. Mac & Arm's believes in fair wages for even the most junior staff members. If you

Miracle On Ladies' Mile   57

do not agree, then perhaps you should consider another place of employment."

Bernard swallowed audibly. "No, that is not necessary, Monsieur Armstrong. I also believe in paying the employees fairly. I will ensure her salary is corrected *immédiatement.*"

"No need," Alex said smoothly. "I have taken care of that. Miss Shipley has also been compensated for the back wages, as it was our mistake."

"Excellent." Gerald sounded relieved. "Then it's settled. Thank you, Felix—"

"One more thing." Alex stood to his full height and thrust his hands in his pockets. "I have observed Miss Shipley in the holiday windows late at night by herself. Not only is this unsafe, it is unfair. I want you and the other designers to assist with the windows over the next few evenings until they are complete. Is that understood?"

Bernard nodded while sweat beaded on his brow. "Yes, indeed. Perfectly, Monsieur Armstrong. I'll see to that straight away."

"You may go."

Bernard started to stand, but Gerald stopped the man's exit by offering his hand to shake. "Thank you, Felix. We do appreciate all your hard work down there. I know you are very busy with the dresses and windows. Let's discuss hiring more staff tomorrow, if you feel it is necessary."

Bernard shook Gerald's hand. "*Merci beaucoup*, Monsieur McCall. It is an honor to work at Mac & Arm's. Truly, it is the finest store in all of New York."

Gerald patted the man's shoulder. "Only because of our employees, Felix. Thank you for your time this afternoon."

After Bernard hurried out, Alex and Gerald retook their seats. Gerald grinned as if the store had just doubled its profit margin. "Well, well, well."

Alex lifted his brows. "Well, what?"

"The return of Miss Shipley."

Alex shuffled a few papers on his desk, avoiding Gerald's keen gaze. The two men had known each other a long time and Alex should've expected this. Still, he didn't care to explain himself. He'd noticed an injustice and had righted it. "I don't know what you're talking about. I learned one of our employees was being mistreated. That's all."

"A matter you'd normally bring to my attention and allow me to handle. You wanted to intimidate Felix. This is personal to you."

"No, it's not. And I'm perfectly capable of handling the employees."

Gerald actually snorted, the bastard. "Remind me how many secretaries you've had in the last five years."

"That's different, and you know it."

"Hmm." Gerald stroked his chin. "Something is different around here, but I'm not sure it has to do with your secretaries."

"You're being ridiculous."

"Am I?"

"Yes. Now get out of here. Some of us have work to do." He could feel the tips of his ears growing hot. Christ, he hadn't blushed since he was a boy. Why was Gerald causing such a stir over this one little meeting? *Because he's right. You hate dealing with disputes and reprimands. You're the numbers and figures man.*

Gerald held up a hand. "I'll go in a minute. Just wanted to say that Sarah has certainly taken a shine to your Miss Shipley. Nice to see the two of them getting along the other day."

"She is not *my* Miss Shipley—and I told Sarah not to bother the design department any longer. The store is not the place for a ten-year-old girl."

"Now, Alex, we don't mind having Sarah about. She cannot get into trouble, not here."

The staff might not mind Sarah here but Alex found it a distraction. Besides, she had mathematics and reading, piano and comportment lessons. She was better off with Mrs. Beadle at home. "It's a place of business, Gerald, not a boarding school."

Gerald held up his hands. "That's your decision, but I think a little time here would do the young girl a bit of good. She might run this store one day, you know."

A burst of pride filled Alex's chest when he thought of his little girl sitting at his desk one day. Hadn't Mrs. Beadle said Sarah had a head for numbers? "She'll likely do a better job than the two of us, that's for certain."

Gerald smirked and rose. "Perhaps this Miss Shipley deserves far more than eight dollars a week. Woman's a dashed miracle worker, if you ask me."

"No one asked you," Alex grumbled.

Gerald's laugh could be heard all the way down the hall as he returned to his office. Alex could only imagine what his partner would say if he knew Alex and Miss Shipley were headed to the Haymarket tonight.

Gerald would probably promote the girl to vice president.

CHAPTER 8

Grace nearly bounced in her seat. She and Alex were on the way to Thirtieth Street and Sixth Avenue, the location of the infamous Haymarket. He'd arrived at her boarding house in a private carriage far more luxurious than anything Grace had ever ridden in before. Stomach fluttering, she dragged a gloved palm over the plush velvet seat. She felt a bit like a princess on her way to the ball.

"Don't forget, you mustn't stray from my side," her prince reminded her for the third time.

She rolled her eyes. "Alex, relax. I promise I won't wander off. Stop worrying."

"Things take place in the Haymarket that no innocent woman should see."

"We had loose women in Farmington. I've also seen them in New York. I'm not completely innocent." She had also kissed a man before and, thanks to an upbringing on a farm, she knew what transpired between couples in bed. Not that she mentioned any of this to Alex.

He held up his hands. "Possibly. However, those experiences won't have prepared you for this level of debauchery."

He was so serious, clearly unhappy about this entire venture. The man hadn't stopped lecturing her since the moment he'd handed her

Miracle On Ladies' Mile 61

into the carriage. She bit her lip and tried for a solemn tone. "I promise not to leave thoroughly corrupted."

"I shall live to regret this."

"Absolutely not! It's going to be good fun. Besides, when was the last time you had any fun? You work longer hours than either McCall or Armstrong, for Pete's sake. I think you need this as much as I do."

He grunted—the male equivalent of not wanting to admit he was wrong. She patted his arm. "We'll have a great evening together. You'll see. When we leave, you shall be thanking me. Besides, we're celebrating. I received a raise today."

"You did?"

"Yes. It was some mix-up with the accounting department when I was hired. See, you're good luck. You said I deserved a raise and then *poof!*" She snapped her fingers. "I received a raise. Plus, I finally had help in the windows today. We're almost finished."

The carriage slowed, swung to the curb, and jerked to a halt. Alex descended then handed her down. He did look a bit like a fairy tale prince. Grumpy, but handsome.

The Haymarket stood across the street, the three brightly lit stories shining like an illicit beacon in the darkness. A jaunty piano tune could be heard from inside even as the Sixth Avenue elevated train rumbled overhead. Well-dressed couples filtered in and out of the entrance, a never-ending revolving door for the biggest party in New York.

Grace tugged Alex's arm. "Come on. Let's go in."

Alex didn't pick up his pace at all. "There's no rush, Grace. The place isn't about to close."

"Says you. I hear it gets raided once a week by the police."

"Only so the police can collect more bribe money from Edward Corey."

"Who's that?" Grace asked, lifting her skirts over the muddy cobblestones as they crossed the street.

"The owner."

"You know quite a bit about the Haymarket. Are you a regular, then?"

"It's been years, but I've visited once or twice."

Had he escorted a woman here? A mistress, perhaps? Her mind spun with this sudden revelation. Did Alex have a mistress? He might still mourn his late wife but that didn't mean the man was celibate. A pang of jealousy lodged under her ribs, and she decided to ignore it. He was here with her tonight, and they would have fun together. She couldn't worry over his past.

A large man sat on a stool at the front door. "Ladies drink for free. Twenty-five cents for gents."

Alex placed the coins in the man's palm and took Grace's elbow. They turned a corner and entered a huge cavernous room. The bar was stationed on the left, while tables crisscrossed the wooden floor. At the stage in the back, a line of women, all wearing brightly colored dresses, had their legs up in the air as they kicked to the gay music. Layers of ruffles and frills were gathered in the front to reveal matching cotton drawers.

Alex leaned down and put his lips near her ear. "Close your mouth. You're liable to attract flies."

"It's...beautiful." Heart pounding, her brain struggled to take it all in. "And amazing. Every bit as exotic as I'd heard. Look at their skirts..."

"Let's find a table. Then, we can watch the action." Grabbing her hand, he pulled her through the crowd toward the side of the dance floor. Small round tables were placed together, so close there was hardly room to squeeze through.

When they found an empty table, he held out a chair. Grace sat, taking care not to crush her bustle. Alex dropped into the opposite seat. Before she could open her mouth to speak, a heavily painted young woman approached them, attention focused entirely on Alex.

"Hello, love," the woman drawled. "Care for a drink? A dance? I could show you upstairs, if you like."

"Just a bottle of champagne and two glasses, please." He withdrew a few bills from his inside coat pocket and handed them over. The woman tucked the money into the bodice of her dress, where her

Miracle On Ladies' Mile

corset could plainly be seen. She winked at Alex and then disappeared.

"What's upstairs?"

Alex grimaced. "Private rooms."

Rooms for...? *Oh.* She glanced up at the ceiling. People were fornicating right above their heads. How fascinating.

"You won't be able to see anything, if that's what you're hoping for," Alex said dryly.

"I know. It's just...so unlike anyplace I've ever been."

"I take it you aren't appalled."

"No. I told you, I'm not completely innocent." He mumbled something under his breath but she couldn't catch it. "What did you say?"

The return of the server girl interrupted them. She quickly poured the drinks and set the bottle down. Draping herself over Alex's shoulder, she leaned in to whisper in his ear. Was the woman propositioning him again?

Another bolt of jealousy rocketed down Grace's spine. How unfair this stranger was able to touch him so intimately, dragging her fingers over his starched shirtfront. Placing her lips on the shell of his ear. What she wouldn't give to trade places with the heavily painted woman right now...

A flash of movement interrupted Grace's thoughts. Alex's hand snatched the server's wrist, which had surreptitiously been making its way into his coat pocket.

"Nice try," he said, gently setting the woman away.

She lifted a shoulder, unaffected at being caught. "Girl's gotta make a living, handsome. Let me know if you change your mind."

Grace's mouth hung open after the server left. "She...she just tried to rob you."

"Perhaps now you'll believe me as to the type of place this is. Are you ready to go home?"

"Not a chance, *handsome.*"

❄

An hour later, Alex had had enough. Grace, on the other hand, seemed to be enjoying herself immensely. Clapping to the music, her eyes were overly bright, and Alex questioned the intelligence of ordering champagne. Their bottle was now empty and he'd only imbibed a glass and a half. He should escort her home before anything untoward happened.

He reached out to touch her arm. "I think it's time to leave."

"Let's dance." An infectious grin split her face.

"No." Bodies were crushed against one another on the dance floor in drunken revelry. Several couples were kissing openly, with no regard for propriety or the stares they garnered. Under no circumstances should Grace join them.

She rose and held out a hand. "Yes, Alex. If you don't dance with me, I'll go by myself."

He frowned even as he stood. During past visits, he'd seen men mistreat women here, groping hands wandering without compunction. The idea of Grace out there alone turned his blood cold. Strange fingers pawing at her waist. Her ribs. Her breasts...

"You promised you'd stay with me." He pointed to her chair. "And I want to stay here."

"I *am* staying with you, but I would like you to dance with me. You're the one who doesn't want to come along." She gripped his arm and pulled.

"That argument is completely illogical."

"Please, Alex?"

The eagerness in her gaze wove a spell, captivating him. He found himself heading toward the melee of dancers in the middle of the floor. She put one hand on his shoulder and clasped his hand with the other. Free hand on her waist, he began leading her in a simple box step around the other couples as best he could.

She kept up, not tripping or moving awkwardly. Their bodies moved fluidly, perfectly, as if they'd done this a hundred times together. He enjoyed the ease of it. The feeling of having her so close.

Miracle On Ladies' Mile   65

When was the last time he'd been dancing? Perhaps right after he and Mary had moved to the city.

"You are an excellent dancer," Grace said.

"As are you. Have you taken lessons?"

"No, we could never afford them. I used to practice with my siblings."

"Not much else to do in Farmington?"

"Definitely not. Only so many times you can watch the grass grow."

A laugh tumbled out of his mouth. "I suppose that's true."

Awareness hummed through his blood. He was so very aware of her skirts rustling about their legs, her hands touching him. Aware of the rise and fall of her chest. Her smell—sweet roses and a hint of paint—burrowed under his skin as his heart pounded a steady rhythm of ardent yearning. God knew why the combination of all these simple things was so thoroughly arousing...

Yet, they were. Disturbingly so.

Blood pooled in his groin, warmth curling through his veins. He stared at the smooth, pale skin of her throat. He'd start his discoveries there, nibbling and testing her soft flesh. Then, he'd advance to the mounds of her breasts, so close now to the fabric of his vest. Lower still, he would discover the color and shape of her nipples, learn the taste of them on his tongue...

He dragged in a deep breath, trying to get himself under control. His cock was already half hard. Any more daydreaming and dancing would soon prove difficult.

A man stumbled behind Grace, bumping her straight into Alex's chest. Alex clasped her hips to steady her as her hands went around his neck. With their bodies flush, there could be no question as to his partial state of arousal. Her lips parted in surprise and she lifted her face. Her blue gaze locked with his, searching for answers he couldn't begin to supply.

Neither of them pulled away. God, he wanted her. He wanted her naked, spread out beneath him, staring up at him with those big eyes that hid nothing. The moment stretched as the revelry continued around them, unnoticed. The noise drowned out the tiny voice of reason in his head insisting he release her. That he stop this madness.

No, not yet.

He wasn't ready to lose this. No woman had made him so crazed, not in forever, a woman who caused him to throw breeding and good sense out the window for a small taste of her. Heat sparked between them and bold feminine fingers began toying with the ends of his hair. Without meaning to, his hands swept over her hips in a gentle caress. When the tip of her tongue emerged, wetting her lips, he couldn't resist the pull. God help him, but he had to kiss this woman. Right the hell now, on the floor of the Haymarket.

He lowered his head. "I'm going to kiss you. I'm going to kiss you right now, right here, unless you stop me."

"Please, Alex."

Those two words unleashed something in him, a bone-deep hunger he thought he'd lost seven years ago. He swooped down to seal his mouth to hers. Her soft lips moved eagerly, urgently, under his, and he clutched her tighter. She didn't shy away or retreat. No, Grace pressed closer and held on.

The unexpected enthusiasm overwhelmed him. He didn't want to scare her, yet he couldn't keep from deepening the kiss and thrusting his tongue past her lips. Slick warmth enveloped him. She tasted of champagne and ebullience, a dangerous, intoxicating combination. She stroked his tongue with her own, exploring, until his head swam. Something dark and profound seeped into his bones, filling up all those empty places long ignored, until he felt a few hundred feet tall.

He hadn't felt this way in a long time. Perhaps ever.

They were jostled once more, and Alex instantly pulled back. Dear God, he'd been mauling her in the middle of the Haymarket. Had he lost his ever-loving mind?

He cleared his throat and dropped his hands, putting space between them. Grace swayed. Her lids blinked slowly while her chest heaved. A flush had bloomed over her lovely skin. The obvious signs of arousal both enticed and frightened him. His cock begged for him to throw up her skirts and feel her delicious wetness on his fingers . . . while his brain ordered him to run straight out the door.

With horror, he realized something else. Not once during that kiss had he thought of his Mary. She hadn't crossed his mind at all. He... he hadn't ever forgotten her before, even during physical intimacies. She normally hovered like a specter in his mind, a reminder of all he'd lost and would never find again.

Appalled, his desire wilted. This was not what he wanted—*who* he wanted—even as logic told him the past was dead and buried.

Grace.

Grace was here now, staring up at him in awe and recognition, as if she'd tested all the men in New York and had settled on him for the rest of her life. He wanted to say, "*No, anyone but me. Choose someone else.*" Not him, a man who had sworn never to marry again. Too much had happened. His heart had already been battered beyond repair. He couldn't let someone in once more, trust and love them, plan on a future together, especially not this trusting girl who had so much joy and laughter inside her. She should have everything, much more than he could ever give her.

Because he would never replace Mary, the mother of his child and the keeper of his soul. Never.

And Grace deserved better.

Alex opened his mouth to tell her as much...and spotted Felix Bernard entering the room.

CHAPTER 9

The room tilted and Grace wondered if the cause was the champagne or Alex's glorious kisses. Then she realized he was tugging her across the floor toward the rear of the Haymarket. "Where are we going?"

Instead of answering, he switched positions to take her left hand instead of her right. He coughed, hunching over as they walked. "Are you all right?" she asked.

The stairs loomed ahead. Was he...? No, he wouldn't dare take her up where the girls entertained their customers. Would he?

A dark thrill skated down her spine.

They went past the stairs, continuing into the darker recesses near the back. There were no doors or windows, so she had no idea what he was about. Was he searching for the kitchen? "Wait," she said, pulling him to a stop. "What are you looking for?"

He cast a glance over her shoulder and then quickly dragged her to a curtained alcove.

Unfortunately, it was occupied.

The curtain parted to reveal a man and woman wrapped around each other. The woman shot them an annoyed glance. "This one's taken, love."

Alex withdrew a few bills from his pocket and held them out to her. "Find another."

She grinned and snatched the money, tucking it in her bodice. "No problem. Come on, sweetheart." Taking her lover's hand, she disappeared, dropping the heavy cloth to leave Alex and Grace in complete darkness.

Her heart kicked in her chest. Was he going to kiss her again? "Alex?"

"Here," he said quietly. His large hand landed on her shoulder. "Do not be scared."

"I'm not scared, just curious about what we are doing behind this curtain." Her hands traveled up his chest, over his silk vest and crisp shirt, skimming the fine wool covering his shoulders. She wound her arms around his neck and pressed close. He was warm and sturdy, an anchor to counterbalance the champagne and excitement bubbling through her. "Did you bring me here to kiss me again?"

"No," he said. The lack of light prevented her from seeing his face, but he sounded...horrified.

"Oh. I assumed... I'm sorry." She started to pull away but he placed his hands on her hips, preventing her escape.

"Wait. I...I thought you might like a moment of privacy." His fingers dug into her waist, as if afraid to let go. "We shouldn't be kissing, though."

"Because you didn't enjoy it? But I thought..." Hardly ladylike to point out she'd felt his arousal during their kiss.

"I enjoyed kissing you." His hands drifted over her rib cage and swept her back. "I enjoyed it a bit too much, honestly."

She could almost make out his features as her eyes began to adjust to the darkness. He was solid and real under her touch. She desperately craved more kissing...more of this strange heat between them. Just *more*.

"There's no one watching us now," she whispered, rising up on her toes and placing a bold kiss on his jaw. "We're all alone."

A shudder went through him. "God, Grace," he rasped. "We shouldn't. You don't even know—"

She put a finger over his lips, preventing him from finishing the sentence. "You won't hurt me, Alex. I'm—"

"Drunk. On champagne."

"No, not any longer. My head may well be muddled but it's not from the drinks."

His nose coasted over her cheek, his breath hot on her skin as he nuzzled her. Then he sighed. "How was I ever to resist you?" His mouth captured hers once more and he kissed her hard. His lips firm and urgent against her mouth, his hands drawing her closer. Trapping her.

Sparks, like little fireflies, flooded her insides. Her skin felt feverish, itchy and tight, barely strong enough to contain the rush of pleasure coursing through her blood. She opened to him without hesitation, certain that she was ready for whatever happened between them. Never had she met anyone like Alex. A decent, intelligent man who unlocked some secret part of her.

His tongue swept into her mouth, teasing and stroking, until she could hardly breathe. She melted into his large frame, shifting closer until they were flush. His arms wrapped around her back, holding her snugly, while he continued to kiss her.

The outside noise fell away, leaving only the two of them, alone, in a private world of temptation and pleasure. Nothing seemed real except for Alex, the strong, capable man kissing her as if he were starving.

And she loved every delirious second of it.

Spinning them, he reversed their positions, slamming into her, pressing her against the wall. He broke off and began dropping fervent kisses along the side of her neck. She panted, chest heaving behind her corset, as he tested and teased her skin with his teeth and tongue. Her hands clutched his shoulders, nails digging into the fabric of his coat, feeling his muscles shift and bunch with his movements.

He continued lower, over her collarbone, and finished with another scrape of his teeth. His palm covered one breast and forced the mound higher, nearly to the top of her modest neckline. He

Miracle On Ladies' Mile

71

nibbled and licked the swell of her breast, and fire swept through her veins, settling between her legs. Her back bowed, silently begging for more.

"You are impossibly lovely and this is beyond reckless," he said between tiny kisses over her décolletage. "But God help me, I do not want to stop."

She thought she'd die if he stopped. The secret place between her legs throbbed in time with her heartbeat, her body racing toward some elusive point in the distance. Needing relief, she arched to align their hips. His arousal, stiff and considerable, rolled against her mound. They both gasped.

He growled an animal-like sound and claimed her mouth once more. She kissed him hard, loving that she had the power to affect him like this. Air washed over her stockings as fabric rustled. In seconds, he had her skirts gathered at her waist. Large fingers soon located the slit in her drawers and she nearly sighed in gratitude. *Yes, touch me where I ache most.*

Without reservation, she widened her legs slightly. Anticipating. He dragged a fingertip over her seam, circling her entrance. "You are so hot. So wet."

He moved then, swirling and rubbing the tiny knot within the folds, driving her out of her mind. Out of her skin. Everything centered in that one spot, every heartbeat, every breath. She was rising, filling, tightening...until it all exploded in a rush of light and sensation. He covered her mouth in a blistering kiss, swallowing her moans, until she stopped shuddering.

Dizzily, she clutched his shoulders as she drifted down. He rested his forehead on her shoulder, his breathing erratic and harsh. She knew he wanted her, but he remained there, unmoving. Tenderness bloomed inside her, and she longed to please him as he'd satisfied her.

She reached for the button on his trousers. "Help me," she whispered. "I don't know what to do." He tried to step back, so she wrapped her fingers in his waistband. "No, Alex. Show me. I want to do this for you."

His big body trembled, yet he said, "I shouldn't. You shouldn't. It's not proper . . . and I am hanging on to my decency by a thread."

"I wouldn't offer if I didn't want this."

Without waiting on his answer, she unfastened his trousers. He held perfectly still as she traced his rigid erection through his underclothes. She pressed with the heel of her hand and his hips jerked, a hiss stealing past his lips. He dove for her mouth, sealing them together, his tongue urgent and greedy against hers. His fingers helped her unbutton the last layer of clothing and then his penis, large and heavy, was in her fist.

"Hold me tight," he told her through labored breaths. "Tighter."

She gripped hard, her fingers clamping down on the soft, steely skin.

"Yes, like that." He moaned and then began to thrust into her grip. "Oh God, Grace."

He moved faster, kissing her roughly. She loved this wild, uninhibited side of him. It was like their own private world behind this curtain where nothing seemed quite real. They weren't two department store employees out for a night at a scandalous dance hall, but merely a man and a woman hungry for each other. Enjoying stolen moments, stolen kisses.

His hand covered hers on his shaft. Hips speeding up, he grunted. He reached inside his coat and withdrew something, but it was too dark to see what. Suddenly, he wrenched away from her and shifted to the side. Eyes closed, he trembled and rode out his orgasm.

He braced himself on the wall with one hand. His head hung down as he caught his breath. "Damn, I did not mean for any of this to happen. Did I spill on you? I tried to catch it all in my handkerchief."

Oh. She hadn't considered that consequence when this started. After a quick examination of her skirts, she answered, "No, I don't believe so."

Silently, he tucked himself back into his combination and adjusted his clothing. He didn't meet her eyes. Even in the dim light, she could see his unhappiness. Stiff movements. Tense muscles. Regret hung on his frame like a frock coat.

"Alex—"

"We should go." He took her hand and parted the curtain. Both of them squinted in the harsh overhead lighting. "Let's get you home."

Shame cast a heavy shadow on Alex's heart as he and Grace crossed the Haymarket's dance floor. She trailed him, saying nothing. He noted, thankfully, that Bernard was nowhere to be seen. Upstairs, perhaps? No telling how long Alex and Grace had been behind that curtain.

Christ, what had he done? It hadn't been planned. He'd tried to keep from touching her, to merely talk. But he hadn't been able to control himself, not when Grace clung to him, whimpering and begging. Her feverish kisses were like the sweetest honey after years of denial.

Still, it was no excuse for what happened. He was an animal. A rutting beast. He'd taken advantage of Grace's naïve willingness, her sweet-natured goodness. Only a reprobate would do something that dishonorable.

When they reached his carriage, he handed her up and quickly followed. The wheels started rolling, and for one insane second, Alex wished to be someone else. Perhaps the man Grace thought him to be, a simple Mac & Arm's employee without towers of responsibility and a daughter to whom he didn't know how to speak. Without a dead wife who'd been the source of his happiness. If he were that man, he and Grace could...explore whatever this was between them.

But there was no erasing the past. There had already been a woman in his life, a woman who'd meant everything, and Alex was no longer a young fanciful man. That man had died seven years ago, and Grace didn't deserve someone so embittered and jaded. She deserved laughter and light. Children. A husband who could love her unconditionally.

"I'll not apologize."

Startled by her words, he glanced over. "Indeed, I believe I owe you the apology."

"No, you don't. We are two adults, Alex, and no one was coerced. What happened was not regrettable."

"You will regret it, I assure you. In time, when you've reflected on this."

"Why are you so certain?"

"One day you'll find a man with whom you wish to have a future, and you'll think back on tonight and long to take it all back."

"And perhaps I won't. You cannot predict the future. No one can. I liked what happened tonight. I am disappointed you don't feel the same."

"Grace—"

"No, I understand." Her voice was hard and clipped. "You are sorry because you think I'm some silly, irresponsible farm girl who cannot possibly know what she wants."

He felt his own anger begin to rise. "No, I'm sorry because tonight was wildly inappropriate. Because I took advantage of you. Because I do not want you to have expectations regarding me."

He'd nearly shouted the last sentence. Grace's beautiful blue eyes went wide, hurt flashing, and then she lowered her lids. "I see," she said quietly, looking away and smoothing her skirts.

He pinched the bridge of his nose. Shit. He'd mangled this. Though what he said was entirely true, he hadn't meant to hurt her feelings.

"Again, you are making assumptions about me. I am not trying to trap you in marriage. This isn't a high society debutante ball. We are merely two friends out enjoying the evening together. At least, we *were* enjoying it."

She was right. His fear of becoming involved in another serious relationship had clouded everything else. Not once had he asked Grace how she felt. What she wanted. He dropped his head back against the velvet seat.

"I enjoyed it," he admitted. "And I would like to remain friends

Miracle On Ladies' Mile

with you, but not the sort of friends who...take advantage of one another. You deserve better, Grace."

"That may be so, but one of the reasons I love living in the city is that I am able to make my own choices. No one tells me what to do or how I should act, what time I need to get up or whether I'm able to skip church on Sunday. I shall decide for myself what I deserve, Alex."

"Fine, but don't say I didn't warn you."

"Now you have me thinking I should rescind that offer of friendship."

He barked a laugh then shook his head, astounded that she could change his mood so quickly. "Please, don't."

"Why? You must have an army of friends, people in your life who care about you."

No, he didn't. He had Gerald, Sarah, and Mrs. Beadle. Since Mary's death he hadn't allowed anyone to get close...until Grace. Not having her in his life at all would crush him. He decided she deserved the truth. "Because there's something about you that fascinates me. You're creative and kind. Attractive and funny. And your laugh can light up a room quicker than Edison."

Her head snapped toward him. From the corner of his eye, he watched a blinding smile transform her face. Something inside Alex's chest tightened.

"Friends, then," she said softly, reaching across to clasp his hand with her gloved fingers.

He exhaled, everything inside him settling, calming, and he didn't let go of her hand until they reached her boarding house.

CHAPTER 10

Grace was not altogether unsurprised when young Sarah Armstrong appeared again the next day.

"Allow me to guess," Grace drawled when the girl showed up in the design department. "Your dire assistance is required with the holiday displays?"

Sarah gave a sheepish smile, dipping her blond head to avoid Grace's gaze. "Lessons are so *boring*. What you do is fun and interesting. Much better than learning arithmetic and Latin."

"Arithmetic is important. You need it for creating dress patterns."

"What about Latin?"

Grace shrugged. "I couldn't say. I suppose you don't need it unless you're going into law or medicine."

"I want to be a dress designer. Like you."

Warmth wrapped around Grace's heart. Still, she forced a stern expression. "You are merely flattering me so I do not squeal on you to your father."

Sarah giggled. "You would not squeal on me. We're friends. Besides, it's true."

Charmer. "Please tell me your governess knows you are here."

"Of course," she said with a roll of her eyes. "Do you think I just walked out of the house without anyone noticing and hailed a hack on my own?"

Well, when put that way, it did seem a bit far-fetched.

"Fine. Gather up those tiny nightingales, please."

For the rest of the morning, Grace and Sarah worked stringing the birds together that would hang from the display window's ceiling. Other members of the design department filtered in, working on their own pieces for *The Nightingale* window. Grace shared her lunch —a small piece of beef, three slices of bread, and a wedge of cheese— with Sarah while they discussed what else the girl was currently studying. "That is a very impressive list," Grace remarked when Sarah had finished with her list of lessons and activities. "When is your time for just fun?"

"I am allowed thirty minutes every afternoon to play with my dolls."

Thirty minutes? That hardly seemed fair. The girl's schedule needn't be so rigid, in Grace's opinion. Children liked spontaneity, the excitement of something new every now and again.

So did adults, for that matter. Like last night. That had certainly been something new and exciting—for the both of them. It had been wonderful, probably the best night of her life. And if Alex chose to be friends and nothing more, then she would always remember their outing at the Haymarket.

Not that she'd stop hoping for more. Perhaps one day he'd find himself ready for another relationship. Grace refused to give up on him so soon. He might not feel as deeply for her as she did for him, but she knew there was something there. She'd seen it in the way he'd looked at her, the way he'd kissed her. The alcove. He just needed more time.

After lunch, Grace took Sarah to her favorite place in the store, the room where all the bolts of fabric were stored. They spent a long time discussing cloth and which fabrics were easier to work with when designing a dress. Sarah declared she would attempt to sew a dress for her doll and asked Grace's opinion on the easiest pattern.

When their lunch break had ended, they headed back to the

workroom. Loud voices carried down the hall.

"I swear, I only took my eye off her for a moment," a female voice said.

"They were just here, *monsieur*. I do not know where—"

Grace and Sarah stepped into the room to discover a crowd had gathered. Every head swung their way. "What's—"

A man stepped forward. *Alex.* Grace started to smile until she noted his thunderous expression. Then she noticed Mr. McCall, Mr. Bernard, the other designers, and Sarah's governess, Mrs. Beadle. Sarah shifted closer and clasped Grace's hand.

Oh no.

"You had everyone worried half to death!" Alex roared at Sarah. The little girl trembled at Grace's side.

Why was... Oh, goodness. *Of course.* Alex was Alexander *Armstrong*, Sarah's father. But...he said he worked all over the store. That he liked furs the best. That he had worked in the children's department...

He'd lied. Not only that, he'd deliberately concealed his identity from her. Why?

Because he doesn't care about you, not in the way you care about him. He hadn't trusted her with the truth, not even after he'd had his hands up her skirts.

Ice slid through her veins, her heart rending like a thin scrap of cotton.

But there was no time for hurt feelings because his attention was entirely focused on Sarah, who cowered at Grace's side.

"I'm sorry, Papa," Sarah mumbled. "I knew Mrs. Beadle wouldn't let me come and I wanted—"

"What you want does not matter," Alex snapped. "Everyone out!"

Mr. McCall began herding the crowd toward the doorway. Grace tried to let go of Sarah's fingers but the young girl held fast, her hand quaking in Grace's. How could she leave the girl to face her angry father alone, especially after all Sarah had shared? Grace decided to stay. Someone needed to help this little girl stand up to Alexander Armstrong.

Miracle On Ladies' Mile 79

Everyone left but the three of them. "Grace, please?" Alex gritted out, tipping his chin to the hall.

"No. I think I'll stay until Sarah asks me to leave."

Alex's shoulders stiffened. Instead of arguing, however, he crossed his arms over his chest. "Sarah, come out from behind Grace's skirts."

The girl took a step to the side, keeping a firm grip on Grace's hand. He stared at his daughter for a long, uncomfortable moment. "How did you get to the store?"

"I hired a hack."

"Alone?"

"Yes."

He closed his eyes in an obvious effort to contain his emotions. "Did you not consider how disappearing would worry Mrs. Beadle? Or the panic I would experience when I learned you were missing?"

"I didn't think anyone would care," she said, her voice shaking. Tears started to roll down the girl's cheeks and a lump rose in Grace's throat. No little girl should have ever thought her father didn't care. She clasped Sarah's hand tighter.

Alex appeared dazed by the answer, as if he'd been punched. "How could you say that? Of course, we care."

"You don't. You care about the store most of all."

"That's not true." He dropped to his haunches and tried to reach for her, but Sarah shrank into Grace. Alex's arm fell but he didn't move away. "I love you, Sarah."

"No, you don't. You hate me because I remind you of Mama. I heard the servants talking about it."

Alex paled and said nothing, too shocked to speak. Grace covered her mouth with her free hand, no idea what to do now. This was a private moment between father and daughter, yet she was here at Sarah's request. Her heart went out to Alex as well, this complicated man who'd confessed he never knew what to say or do around children. Clearly, he'd been speaking about Sarah, his small daughter who only wanted to spend time with him.

And that made her heart hurt for both of them.

She was still furious with him, but she had to help Sarah.

Running a palm over the girl's hair, she said, "Sarah, I'm certain your father loves you very much. He—"

Sarah tore free from Grace, her delicate face splotchy and wet. "No, he doesn't. He never comes home and he doesn't want to see me. I wish I'd never been born!" She raced from the room in a flutter of white petticoats.

The clock on the wall ticked in the silence. Alex stared at the floor, still kneeling, his face pale and shoulders stooped in defeat. Grace did not rush to fill the silence. She rather thought he deserved his misery, this man who'd lied to her and broken a ten-year-old girl's heart. Not only that, she wasn't certain she could reassure him, not any longer. Whatever friendship they might have had was ruined by his deception.

Mrs. Beadle poked her head in the doorway. "I'll take Miss Sarah home, if that's all right with you, sir."

That seemed to shake Alex out of his reverie. He rose and shoved his hands in his trouser pockets. "Yes, please. And thank you, Mrs. Beadle."

The governess disappeared, leaving Alex and Grace alone once more. Quite a different ending to the day from what she'd intended. Instead of feeling hopeful, she felt heartsick for poor Sarah. Heartsick for herself. *You're too trusting, Grace. Don't let those big city boys take advantage of you.*

Too late, Grace wanted to tell her mother. She'd failed spectacularly at that piece of advice. It wasn't too late, however, to tell Alex exactly what she thought.

Alex stared at the door, his throat tight. That had not happened how he'd planned. At all.

"You need to apologize to her," Grace said quietly, gaining his attention. "Spend time with her, regardless of how you feel. Your feelings no longer matter, in fact. To ignore her is the height of selfishness. If what she believes is true, that you avoid her because of your

Miracle On Ladies' Mile 81

grief, then you must find a way to move past that grief. If you cannot, go let her live with relatives."

He nodded, certain she was right. Sarah was suffering. Sarah, his only child. His *daughter*. And she thought he hated her. Christ, he was a shit.

"So you're Alexander Armstrong."

Oh, God. He'd forgotten. *You owe her the truth, you bastard.* "Yes. I'm sorry I didn't tell you."

"Why lie to me? What did that possibly gain you?"

Because I wanted you to see me differently. "It just felt...easier. When people learn who I am, the knowledge changes how they act."

"When they learn about your money, you mean."

"Yes, among other things."

She huffed a dry, pained laugh. "I must have sounded pretty stupid going on about my financial woes." Her eyes flew open. "The raise! Of course. How stupid of me. You did that, not Mr. Bernard."

He rushed to explain, desperate for her to understand. "You earned that money, Grace. He should have started you at the higher salary."

She shook her head as if she didn't believe him. "And the help with the holiday windows. That's why the rest of the designers suddenly began to work on them, because the boss ordered it."

"They should've been doing that all along."

"Everyone knew who you were but me. I can only imagine what it must have looked like, the poor shop girl throwing herself at the storeowner. Mercy, what a cliché I am."

Alex didn't pretend to be oblivious to what she meant. A popular musical had been staged the year before about shop girls doing precisely that. "I never thought you had an agenda, Grace."

"Only because you lied to me about who you were." Her hands clenched into fists at her side. "What about everyone else? Did Mr. Bernard know?"

"I'm not certain," Alex hedged, not wanting to lie to her even more.

Her eyes narrowed. "What does that mean?"

"I saw him last night at the Haymarket. I don't know if he saw us together. I tried..." He trailed off, intensely wishing they weren't having this conversation. That she was still staring up at him as if he were the best man in New York City. The one with whom she wanted to kiss and dance, the one to take her to seedy dance halls. Instead, she was looking at him as if she'd never seen him before. As if they were strangers.

"The curtain." She put a hand to her stomach and squeezed her eyes shut. "That's what you were trying to do. You wanted to hide me, not kiss me. Oh, God."

Spinning on her heel, she started for the door. *She's leaving.* No, he had to make her understand. She had misinterpreted everything. Yes, he'd lied about his name but that was it. Everything else between them had been real, so real it had terrified him.

He lunged forward and took hold of her arm. "Grace, wait. Allow me to explain."

She ripped her arm out of his grasp. "Let me go. You're not a nice man. And you are a liar. Besides, you should stop worrying about me and apologize to your daughter instead."

His heart twisted, pain and misery leaking into his chest. He was losing her—for good. "I'm sorry for lying. And I shall speak to Sarah this evening when I return home."

"After you've left her to cry all day? God, Alex. Go *now*. Reassure her that you love her as soon as possible. Besides, we're done. I have nothing else to say to you. Ever."

He didn't care for the condescension in her voice, as if this course of action was obvious to everyone but him. Obviously, he'd failed Sarah. The entire Mac & Arm's staff would be discussing his failure soon, thanks to the crowd gathered a few moments ago, but he didn't need advice from anyone. "I cannot leave in the middle of the day. Not to mention, how I raise Sarah is not up for debate or discussion. It's my decision, not yours."

"A shame it's not my decision because you are treating her terribly. If I were her mother—"

His skin broke out in flames, the anger swift and fierce, and he latched onto it, grateful to feel something other than shame or misery. "But you're not. You are *not* her mother. Her mother is dead, so do not presume to admonish me."

The words were said with more vehemence than he expected and his ire deflated. He instantly wished to retract his outburst so he could prevent the hurt that flickered over her face. "I apologize. That was unnecessarily harsh."

Grace drew herself up, squaring her shoulders. "No, you are right. I am not her mother. Fortunate for you, I suppose, because I would have shaken you into being the kind of father Sarah deserves ages ago."

She stepped toward the exit, putting more distance between them. "So you may now safely return to ignoring her. I won't interfere any longer."

"What are you saying?"

"I'm saying you needn't worry about me causing trouble in your life." She raised her chin. "We are no longer friends—or anything else."

A panic he hardly recognized swept through him. He didn't want to lose her. It was so obvious to him now that Grace was much more than a friend. She was the person he looked forward to seeing, the person he needed to hear laugh each day. The woman he craved in his bed each night. He wasn't ready to give any of that up. "Grace, I'm sorry I lied about my name. But it shouldn't matter. You know me— the man I am inside—perhaps better than most."

"Wrong. You definitely are not the man I thought I knew." She opened the door that led to the hall. "And I don't care for the one I've just met."

The door slammed behind her and Alex could only stand there, dazed. In the span of moments, he'd just lost the two most important females in his life. His daughter, the other half of his heart, and Grace, the woman who'd charmed her way into his soul. He had to fix both relationships through whatever apologies and changes were required...or he'd never survive it.

CHAPTER 11

Alex stood outside Sarah's door, listening. He couldn't hear anything, though Mrs. Beadle had assured him his daughter was inside. "Poor lamb cried all the way home," the governess had reported, causing guilt and self-loathing to lodge in Alex's throat.

He knocked. "Sweetheart, may I come in?"

No sound emerged. She couldn't be asleep. He'd taken Grace's advice and rushed straight home, arriving mere moments after Sarah and Mrs. Beadle. "Sarah, please."

She continued to ignore him, so he tried the latch. Locked. He withdrew his master key, unlocked the door, and pushed his way inside. The room was dim, with only a low fire burning in the grate. The overhead light remained off.

She was curled up on top of the mattress, facing away from the door. She didn't move or speak as he approached. He stood at the side of her bed, wondering where to start.

He never comes home and he doesn't want to see me.

Christ, how that hurt. No matter what, he had to be a better father. Mary would have been very disappointed. She had wanted Sarah to be raised with love and kindness. Laughter and joy. Not ignored and made to feel an afterthought.

You hate me because I remind you of Mama.

God above, what had he done?

All these years he thought he'd been hiding his grief, burying it in his work. Now his daughter thought he hated her. How could he ever repair this?

Slipping off his frock coat, he threw it on a nearby chair before stretching out on the bed next to his daughter. He folded his hands beneath his head and stared at the canopy overhead. He could hear Sarah breathing, her small body rising and falling in an erratic rhythm. Was she still crying?

"I'm sorry." His voice sounded like rough gravel in the quiet space. "It's not enough. It'll never be enough, but I never intended to hurt you."

Her only reaction was a sniffle. He soldiered on.

"I don't hate you. I could never, ever hate you." He swallowed. "I do miss your mother, that's true. I miss her every single day, but that doesn't mean I don't love you or care about you."

"Then why don't you want to see me?"

The whispered question held so much vulnerability, so much hurt. He didn't have the heart to admit to the real reason, that she reminded him of Mary, because that knowledge would only confirm what Sarah suspected and cause her more anguish. So he went with a version of the truth. "I don't know much about little girls. I never had any sisters. Your mother, she was better at this. She knew exactly what to do, how to always make you feel better. You hardly ever left her side."

Sarah slowly rolled toward him, her red-rimmed eyes curious and bright. "Really?"

Alex nodded. "Yes. You held onto her skirts, ran on little legs to catch her. No matter where she went, you were right there beside her." The memory warmed his chest, but not with the sharp-edged grief he usually experienced. No, this was a dull ache tinged with fondness. Strange.

"I wish I remembered her."

God, that admission made him ache, both for Sarah and for Mary. His wife had so desperately wanted to watch their daughter grow up.

He blew out a long breath. "I can tell you anything you'd like to know. Whenever you wish."

"What was her favorite color?"

"Yellow."

"Mine's brown."

"Brown?" He shifted to see her face. "Really?"

"It's the color of my favorite horse."

"You have a favorite horse? What's his name?"

"Her, and it's Buttons."

"Because her eyes look like buttons?"

"No. I just liked the name."

He chuckled. "Your mother was scared to death of horses. I couldn't hardly get her on one."

"She was? That's sad. I love to ride."

He didn't know any of this. "Do you ride in the park?"

"Yes. There are lots of pretty paths."

"Perhaps you could show me one day."

"You would go riding with me?"

"Of course," he said easily. "From now on, you and I are going to find things we both like to do together."

"Cross your heart?"

He sucked in a breath. Grace had said the same once, back when they first met. Grace, who now hated him. Focusing on Sarah, he ran a fingertip gently over the end of her nose. "Cross my heart, sweetheart."

"Why do you look so sad all of a sudden?"

Her perceptiveness startled him and he considered lying. However, the only way to build a relationship with Sarah was to talk to her, and he figured she deserved the truth. Especially since she obviously liked Grace as much as he did. "Well, that's something Grace said when she once asked me to make a promise."

"I like Grace. Don't you like her, too?"

You could say that. He'd only just realized how much, right before she said her piece and walked away. Alex had every intention of apologizing to her and asking her to play a prominent role in his life, but there was no guarantee he could convince her. Perhaps it was best to break this to Sarah gently, so she wasn't disappointed later on. "Yes, I do. Immensely. But I'm afraid she doesn't care for me any longer."

"Why not?"

"I lied to her."

"Mrs. Beadle says it's not ladylike to lie."

"It's not gentlemanly either. Without meaning to, I hurt Grace's feelings sort of like how I hurt your feelings, and I'm afraid she doesn't wish to speak to me any longer."

"You must apologize to her. Otherwise, she won't give me the Snow Princess dress."

"What dress?"

"The Snow Princess dress. It's silver and beautiful and the prettiest dress ever created. She said she would give it to me, if Mr. Bernard said it was all right."

If Bernard wanted to keep his job, he'd agree. Grace, on the other hand, was another matter. He'd need to speak with her, ensure she would keep this promise to Sarah. "I'm certain Grace will give you the dress, even if she's cross with me."

"I hope so. She is my friend. You should still apologize to my friend, because it's the proper thing to do."

"I did apologize—repeatedly—but it didn't make her any less angry. And she is my friend, too."

"Perhaps she just needs time. When I get angry, sometimes I feel better in a few hours."

Wise words from his ten-year-old daughter. Alex smiled and pushed an errant lock of blond hair off her face. "Are you feeling better now?"

"Yes, because you're here."

As if they'd done it a hundred times before, he opened his arms and Sarah shifted to snuggle her small body next to him. Surprised at how natural this seemed, he exhaled and wrapped her in a hug. He pushed all the other thoughts and memories away, thinking only of his daughter and this moment right now. He placed a kiss to the top of her head. "That is the nicest thing you could've said. I truly am sorry, Sarah."

They stayed there a long moment. He hadn't held her like this since she was a toddler, when the three of them used to cuddle in bed. Why hadn't he realized he could still do it with just his daughter?

"May I visit the store again one day?" she asked.

"Yes, if Mrs. Beadle agrees. You gave her quite a scare today."

"I know. She cried on the way home. I apologized."

"Good. Would you like it if I returned home for supper each evening?'

"Yes. I hate eating with Mrs. Beadle. She makes me eat everything whether I like it or not, even cheese."

"You don't like cheese?" Mary had adored cheeses of all kinds.

"No, especially not the smelly kind."

She is so different. Why did I not see this before? Because he'd never given her a chance.

His eyes burned with regret, the hundreds of wasted hours that could've been spent with Sarah. He would do better by her—and also by Grace. He wasn't ready to give up on her yet either.

A man watched her from the other side of the glass.

This time, however, Grace recognized him.

Five days ago Grace had quit Mac & Arm's. Mr. Bernard had accepted her resignation with pity in his eyes. That pity was precisely why Grace had to quit. No doubt everyone on the store's staff had discussed her humiliation.

Before she left, Mr. Bernard had surprised her by contacting Parker's Department Store across town to recommend her. After Mr. Bernard praised Grace's efforts on the holiday windows, Mr. Parker had hired Grace immediately.

So now she stood in another glass box, this time arranging a nativity scene. Her supervisor at Parker's wasn't worried about secrecy, so the windows remained uncovered, leaving Grace to enjoy the view. At least, up until a few moments ago.

Alex was here. Right outside the window, just a few feet away. This was the third day he'd come to the windows. She had no idea how he'd found her, but he didn't attempt to talk to her. He merely lingered on the sidewalk, his hands stuffed in trouser pockets while watching her until she finished. When she departed, she always found a hack waiting to take her home, the driver already compensated for the journey. A nice gesture on Alex's part but too late to salvage what had once sparked between them. He'd deceived her and she couldn't forgive that.

Just as with the other days, she didn't acknowledge him. What was there to say? Not even his tired expression and the dark circles under his eyes could sway her.

That didn't mean she wasn't aware of him, however. Her skin pebbled and itched under his intense brown gaze, causing her hands to tremble and perspire. What did he expect, that she would forgive him for lying about his identity? And if she did, what then? He wasn't ready to let another woman into his heart, not even his own daughter, for god's sake. Grace couldn't be friends—or whatever—with a man so closed off, so unfeeling.

He hadn't been unfeeling that night at the Haymarket.

Heat prickled along her neck at the memory. The way he'd held her, his kisses...she had certainly witnessed a different side to Alexander Armstrong. Yet that wasn't enough, not considering he'd lied to her from the very start.

She worked with quiet efficiency, desperate to escape his attention as quickly as possible. When she finally left, she expected to see a hack waiting at the curb.

She found Alex instead.

Part of her wanted to disappear back inside the store, but she stood her ground. She'd done nothing wrong, so why should she hide? Moreover, part of her was curious. Why was this man so determined to follow her about? Hadn't he done enough damage?

Blood pumping hotly, she marched toward him, ready to put an end to this. His dark stare tracked her approach like a hunter stalking its prey. "Hello, Grace—"

"Why are you here?" She put her hands on her hips. "I don't know what you hope to accomplish, but you need to stay away."

He grimaced. "I can't. I tried. I...I want to explain. I need you to understand."

"Why?" He sighed but didn't answer, so she continued. "You haven't been honest with me about anything. Why should I believe a word you say?"

"I only lied to you about my position at the store. Everything else was quite real, Grace, including the way I feel about you."

She blinked. Was he implying he had feelings for her—friendly feelings—or something more serious? Her heart skipped in her chest, but she strangled the gleam of hope with simple pragmatism. He couldn't mean anything more than a friendship and any chance of that had been lost when he lied to her. "You feel guilty, no doubt. In a few weeks, you'll forget all about me."

"Not a chance. I wish it were so easy. I can't stop thinking about you, about how much I miss your laugh and your smile. Your honesty and optimism. You're the first woman in a very long time who's made me feel like I'm not dead inside."

"I don't even know you. Where you live, with whom you are friends. What you like for breakfast or your favorite place in the city."

"Fifth Avenue and Eighty First Street. Gerald is my only friend. I usually have a buttered roll and coffee, and wherever you are."

The compliment warmed her, wrapping around her insides, and her ire melted a tiny fraction. "Alex . . ."

He must have sensed the chink in her armor, because he reached out to take her hand. His fingers were gentle. Reverent, as if she were something precious. "I can't lose you, Grace."

She swallowed hard but didn't pull away. "You never had me. Not when there were lies between us. How am I supposed to reconcile the man I met from the great Alexander Armstrong? I don't know if I can do that."

"Why not? We are not so different. I didn't grow up with all this

Miracle On Ladies' Mile

—" He gestured to the fancy carriage behind him. "I grew up in a small town with very little. I remember what it was like to worry about money."

She took her hand back and crossed her arms over her chest. "Yet, you purposely kept that information from me. You thought I would try to trap you because you're rich."

"No. I . . ." He let her go and dragged a hand down his face. "Have you ever tried on a coat that is too small? It pulls across your shoulders and back, wrapping you up, choking you, like everything is closing in on you? I felt that way every day before meeting you. But when I was with you, I could let all the other worries and problems fall away. With you, there's no too-small coat pulling on me. You fit me perfectly."

A lump formed in her throat. Had anyone ever said something so sweet before? She pressed her lips together, savoring the kind words. "But you had to know I would be furious when I found out."

"I wanted to tell you, I did. I couldn't bring myself to do it, though. I couldn't bring myself to ruin what was building between us, something meaningful and special. You're like no one else I've ever met, Grace."

"I don't like being lied to."

"I'm sorry. I'll apologize as many times as you need to hear it— and I'll tell you anything you want to know from now on."

"Anything?"

"Yes. Anything, no matter how personal."

"Did Sarah forgive you?"

He glanced down at his shoes and nodded. "I hope so. I've apologized to her and we are working on building our relationship. She's taken me riding the past two mornings."

"She has taken you?"

His lips curved into a fond smile. "It's mostly me trying to keep up with her in the park. She's quite an accomplished rider."

"I'm glad. The more time you spend with her, the easier it will be."

"I'm discovering that. She misses you."

She couldn't hold back a smile at that news. They hadn't spent much time together but she'd become fond of the girl. "I'd like to see her again, if it's all right with you. Perhaps here at Parker's."

He scowled at the building behind her. "You're not seriously going to keep working here, are you?"

"Well, I'm not coming back to Mac & Arm's. So yes, I thought I might."

"You have to come back. Both Gerald and Mr. Bernard are furious with me, and I miss having you nearby."

The thought of walking through the store, everyone staring at her, laughing . . . She winced. "No, it's too embarrassing. The poor shop girl chasing the boss—who, by the way, never told her he was the boss." She shook her head vehemently. "I cannot."

"No one knows any of that. They believe you were friends with Sarah, that's all. Our conversation remained private. Only Gerald suspects your resignation to be a result of personal issues between the two of us."

Even one person was too many. "I'm sorry. I cannot." She searched his handsome face, the memories of their time together like jagged shards in her chest. How she wished things were different, that he hadn't lied. That there had been honesty and respect between them. That there could have been something lasting, something real.

But wishing didn't make it true.

Regret burned in her throat, each breath a painful endeavor. "Thank you for coming here, for everything you said. However, I think it's best if we don't see each other again."

"Grace, please—"

"I can't." She patted his lapel. Her fingertips lingered to prolong the contact. "Good-bye, Alex."

She left him standing there, his imposing silhouette larger-than-life in the dim light, and started walking home. It was time to put aside her girlish daydreams filled with this handsome man and his fiery kisses.

It was time to get back to real life.

CHAPTER 12

Christmas Eve Eve

The sound of sniffling caught Grace's attention.

Her head snapped up from the dress she was altering to find Sarah Armstrong standing in the Parker's Department Store basement, tears streaming down the young girl's face. Alex's daughter had taken to visiting Grace here two or three times a week. They discussed design and fabrics, and the Parker's staff was always grateful for another helping hand, even the small kind. The topic of Alex had only been raised once and, after Grace's lackluster response, it thankfully hadn't been resurrected.

She shoved aside her sewing, jumped up, and rushed to the girl's side. "Sarah! What's wrong? What happened?"

"I hate him, Grace. I don't want to go back there."

Oh, no. Based on Sarah's happy mood recently, Grace assumed things between father and daughter had improved. Poor Sarah. Swallowing her anger and disappointment at Alex, Grace wrapped the girl in a tight embrace. "Tell me what happened. Perhaps it's not as bad as you think."

"It's awful. I ran away. I don't want to live with him any more. I thought perhaps I could come and live with you?"

Grace blinked. "Sarah, your father would be heartbroken if you left. I know it hasn't been easy between you but you must give him more time."

Sarah dragged in a shuddering breath, her small frame trembling against Grace. "I don't want to go back. You cannot make me."

Grace cast a quick glance at the clock. Goodness, it was nearly five o'clock, when she would leave for the day. "Does Mrs. Beadle know you're here?"

Sarah shook her head and Grace's heart sank. The governess and Alex would be beside themselves with worry. "Listen, I'll take you home and speak to your governess. There must be something we can do to make things better."

"Mrs. Beadle is visiting her sister. I was with Papa at the store."

She'd run away from Mac & Arm's? Good Lord, Alex must be frantic. "Sarah, I must take you back to your father. He's likely worried about you but I promise I won't leave until I know you're all right."

"Do you promise?"

Grace hugged her tighter. "I promise."

She stood, grabbed Sarah's hand, and started toward the exit. Grace was probably dreading this encounter every bit as much as Sarah. An uncharitable thought, considering this was about Sarah and not about *them*, but she had avoided Mac & Arm's since she quit. Everything there was a reminder of Alex, from the store windows outside to the basement. Even the sight of a stepladder caused her to nearly burst into tears these days.

She sighed. Really, what else did she have to do tonight? Her lonely apartment would still be waiting when she finished. She'd have one quick conversation with Alex, make certain Sarah would be fine, and then go straight home, where she would eat copious amounts of fudge and try to forget how much she missed him.

Because she did miss him—terribly. Her chest ached so much on some days that she considered driving to the store, storming into his

Miracle On Ladies' Mile

office, and demanding he tell her what he'd meant that day. *With you, there's no too-small coat pulling on me. You fit me perfectly.* Had he been angling for her friendship...or her heart?

Maybe she'd given up on him too soon. Maybe if she'd given him more time he would have figured out what he wanted. But that wasn't fair to her. She already *knew* what she wanted—and that was Alex. Forever and always.

She pushed that aside as they found themselves on the street. *What's done is done and you can't ever go back.* Her grandmother had been right.

A familiar black carriage waited at the street. "Is that your father's carriage?"

"Yes."

"Good girl. At least you didn't take a hack this time."

Sitting in Alex's carriage, she was surrounded by the scent of his woodsy cologne. Her heart couldn't take it. Why hadn't she insisted they take a hack or a streetcar, any mode of transportation that wouldn't remind her of him?

Sarah was quiet on their journey across town. Grace made a few attempts to learn what had caused her to run away tonight but Sarah wouldn't tell her.

Finally they arrived at Mac & Arm's. The towering building, lit up for the season, stood proudly on the corner, its holiday windows the talk of New York. Crowds had gathered outside to see the displays and Grace's chest filled with pride. She had done those.

She tried to focus on that accomplishment as they headed toward the store, instead of thinking of the store's co-owner.

There seemed to be an additional crowd gathered around the *Thumbelina* window. That was strange. It was beautiful, of course, but she wasn't certain it warranted a crush. Peeking over the crowd, she saw a man standing inside it.

Her breath lodged in her throat. *Alex.* Tall and handsome, he was dressed in a fitted dark gray wool suit and lilac-colored silk vest, his body bent at the waist as he examined the edges of the window. What on earth was he doing in there?

"Are you certain I cannot come and live with you?" Sarah asked.

Grace looked down. She'd forgotten for a brief moment that the young girl was there. "You should stay and work things out with your father, Sarah. Come along. Let's go talk to him."

Stomach fluttering with nerves, she waved to the night guard to let them in as the store had just closed. Once inside, she and Sarah went toward the holiday windows. Toward Alex.

The display door was unlocked, so Grace steeled herself and stepped inside. "Alex, I have Sarah—"

The second Alex lifted his head, Sarah's hand ripped from Grace's grip and the display door slammed. It all happened so quickly that Grace struggled to understand. Sarah was on the outside of the window, on the other side of the door. Why?

Her gaze flew to Alex, who was coming toward her, his mouth turned into a frown. His face looked thinner, his cheekbones more pronounced. Hair fell to his collar, giving him a rumpled appearance. Still, he was the most beautiful man she'd ever seen.

The latch on the door engaged, locking them in.

Alex immediately reached for the knob. When it wouldn't budge, he threw a fist onto the door. "Sarah, unlock this right now. Whatever your intentions, this is not a good idea."

"You two need to talk." Sarah's voice was muffled through the wood. "You need to make up."

Grace joined Alex at the locked door. "Sarah, this is serious. You cannot keep us locked in here. Come now, let us out."

"No," came the small voice. "You're both miserable, unwilling to even mention the other's name. I'm tired of seeing you both unhappy. Apologize, or whatever, so you'll be happy again."

"That is not how this works, young lady." Alex banged a fist on the door. "I am your father and I am telling you to open this door."

"I'm leaving and I am not returning until you two are friends again."

"Sarah," Alex warned. "Open this now."

No answer. Alex continued to glare at the door but there was no response from Sarah. Grace sighed, picked up the hem of her skirt,

Miracle On Ladies' Mile

97

and sat on a giant toadstool. She tried to ignore the many pairs of eyes watching them from the other side of the glass. "You might as well get comfortable. No telling when she'll be back."

Alex rested his forehead on the door briefly then straightened. "I apologize. Gerald said there was a leak in one of the windows and asked me to come down and investigate. I had no idea Sarah was coming to the store tonight, let alone that she would lock us in here together."

"Allow me to guess? The two of you didn't fight and she never ran away?"

"No. We've been doing very well together, actually. Until now, that is."

"Clever scamp. She showed up at Parker's and told me she ran away again. That she hated living with you and wouldn't go back. I insisted on bringing her here to you. I wonder how long the little charlatan plans on keeping us in here."

"The guard will let us out before we run out of air, if nothing else. Sarah is incredibly stubborn. She'd likely leave us here all night."

"She is very stubborn. I've noticed when I give her a task that she sees it through until the end and won't accept any help whatsoever."

Alex's mouth curved. "Mary was exactly the same way."

It was the first time he'd mentioned his wife so casually. Interesting. What else might he open up about? "And what did Sarah inherit from you?"

"A love of being outdoors, riding and exploring. A head for numbers. A sweet tooth."

Grace smiled. "Those are all admirable traits to pass along to a child."

"No doubt I've given her some less desirable ones as well. Like the ability to hurt the people we most care about."

The meaning was not lost on her. "Alex . . ."

"I did not say it for sympathy." He put his back against the wall and crossed his legs at the ankles. "However, it's true—and I do not blame you for never wanting to see me again."

It sounded so harsh put that way. "I *want* to see you, but it hurts too much."

"I wish I could go back and do it all differently. I'd introduce myself properly. Escort you about town and buy you dinner at the fanciest restaurants. Take you to the opera. Give you jewels. Whatever you wanted."

She straightened, her shoulders tightening. "I don't need any of those things. Is that what you think would win me over?"

"No, but perhaps I'd like to show you off. Give you adventures. I'd give you everything, Grace."

"All I ever wanted was the truth. I thought you were just a clerk when I fell—" She snapped her jaw shut, biting off the disastrous words that nearly tumbled out of her mouth.

But she'd said enough. Alex took three long strides to close the distance between them. "What were you about to say?"

She bit her lip and stared at the wall. She couldn't admit it, not now. That she'd tumbled head over heels for a man whose last name she hadn't known seemed ridiculous.

Gentle fingers touched her jaw, bringing her gaze to meet his as he swept a lock of hair behind her ear. The tenderness in his eyes weakened her knees. "Were you going to say you fell for me? Because I fell for you, too. I never meant for it to happen but it did. Now I want to learn everything about you and tell you everything in return, no matter how good or bad. We need time to learn each other without the deception between us, and that is all I'm asking for. Please, give me more time. Let me court you, as I should have from the beginning."

She had missed him so terribly. The last few weeks had been excruciating. Part of her longed to give him another chance, but a voice in her head cautioned her. She had to be certain. "You promise to be truthful from now on?"

"Always," he said quickly. "Without equivocation."

"I want to pay my own way. No extravagant gifts, either."

"Fine."

"Also, I don't want to come back to Mac & Arm's just yet."

Miracle On Ladies' Mile 99

Confusion washed over his features. "Why not? We have a better reputation than Parker's Department Store."

"Yes, that's true, but you are one of the owners. I need to create a career for myself. The head designer at Parker's has agreed to let me design a few dresses for next fall."

"Fair enough." He shifted closer, cupping her neck with one large hand. His dark eyes glowed with emotion. "But consider it for the future. I liked having you in my building."

"Fair enough," she echoed, tilting her face up. Heat rolled off his body, and she longed to kiss him again. She licked her lips. "Then I agree to be courted."

A grin spread over his face as he bent his head. "I am going to win you over, Grace Shipley."

"I look forward to your efforts, Alexander Armstrong."

He dipped closer then seemed to realize something, his head shooting up. Thirty or forty people surrounded the window, their avid gazes locked on Alex and Grace. Alex released her and went to the electric outlet. With one mighty pull, he unplugged all of the cords. Darkness descended in the window, resulting in complaints from several spectators.

Grace quickly forgot about them because Alex was back, wrapping her in his arms and kissing her hard, like he'd been starving for her. His lips, coaxing and needy, slid over hers to ignite a fire in her belly. How she'd yearned for this, the sparks in her blood that only Alex could create. Her fingers curled around the base of his neck and into his hair as he dragged her closer. She hoped he never let her go.

A clapping sound penetrated her brain. She broke off the kiss, lungs heaving. Turning toward the window, she found only Sarah and Mr. McCall standing there, applauding. They must have shooed the rest of the crowd away during the kiss. Her face went up in flames and she tried to step away, but Alex's grip tightened. He jerked a thumb at his partner, and Mr. McCall wrapped an arm around Sarah's shoulders, gently steering her out of the line of sight.

Alex turned back to Grace. His mouth descended once again.

"They can wait. I'm not done enjoying my favorite Christmas present yet."

"Me?"

"You," he confirmed and proceeded to steal her breath with a kiss full of possibility and hope.

THE END

Want more Gilded Age romance? Check out <u>A DARING ARRANGEMENT</u>, the first book in the Four Hundred Series from Avon Books...

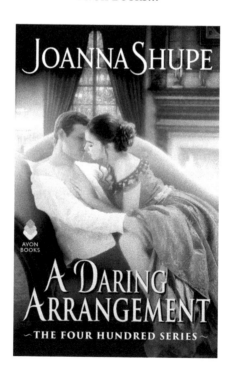

Set in New York City's Gilded Age, Joanna Shupe's Avon debut introduces

Miracle On Ladies' Mile

an English beauty with a wicked scheme to win the man she loves—and the American scoundrel who ruins her best laid plans...

Lady Honora Parker must get engaged as soon as possible, and only a particular type of man will do. Nora seeks a mate so abhorrent, so completely unacceptable, that her father will reject the match—leaving her free to marry the artist she loves. Who then is the most appalling man in Manhattan? The wealthy, devilishly handsome financier, Julius Hatcher, of course...

Julius is intrigued by Nora's ruse and decides to play along. But to Nora's horror, Julius transforms himself into the perfect fiancé, charming the very people she hoped he would offend. It seems Julius has a secret plan all his own—one that will solve a dark mystery from his past, and perhaps turn him into the kind of man Nora could truly love.

Check out A DARING ARRANGEMENT!
Published by Avon Books/Harper Collins

ACKNOWLEDGMENTS

Thank you so much for reading Alex and Grace's holiday story. This was a lot of fun for me to write. Holiday window displays were a Gilded Age-era invention so I couldn't resist using them. The first American department store display was at Macy's in New York City in 1874 with scenes from Harriet Beecher Stowe's "Uncle Tom's Cabin."

A million thanks to my awesome critique partners and writing pals who make this writing gig such a joy. Also thanks to the Gilded Lilies on Facebook who share my enthusiasm for this time period and romance. You ladies are the best!

Many hands helped make this story legible, including my two editors, Felicia Murrell and Sabrina Darby. My thanks to them both, as well as my go-to beta readers, Michele, Julie, and Diana, who make everything better.

Thanks to my husband and my family, who are my biggest cheerleaders, as well as my daughters, who never complain when they repeatedly get chicken nuggets and pizza for dinner.

ABOUT THE AUTHOR

Award-winning author JOANNA SHUPE has always loved history, ever since she saw her first Schoolhouse Rock cartoon. Since 2015, her books have appeared on numerous yearly "best of" lists, including *Publishers Weekly, The Washington Post,* Kirkus Reviews, Kobo, and BookPage.

She currently lives in New Jersey with her two spirited daughters and dashing husband.

Sign up here for Joanna's newsletter to be notified of releases, news, sales, events, and giveaways!

Connect with Joanna:
www.JoannaShupe.com

facebook.com/joannashupeauthor
twitter.com/joannashupe
instagram.com/joannashupe

ALSO BY JOANNA SHUPE

The Uptown Girls Series

The Rogue of Fifth Avenue

The Prince of Broadway

The Devil of Downtown

Anthologies

How the Dukes Stole Christmas

Duke I'd Like to F...

The Four Hundred Series

A Daring Arrangement

A Scandalous Deal

A Notorious Vow

The Knickerbocker Club Series

Tycoon

Magnate

Baron

Mogul

Wicked Deceptions Series

A Courtesan Duchess

The Harlot Countess

The Lady Hellion

Lightning Source UK Ltd.
Milton Keynes UK
UKHW020019101221
395394UK00010B/2299